TOWER of SHADOWS

ONCE UPON A WICKED VILLAIN

CANDACE ROBINSON
AMBER R. DUELL

For those who can see there is good in a villain

ROZLYN

Once upon a time, a madam of a brothel took in an abandoned little girl, showing her the care and love that her parents never had. The girl was allowed to make her own choices—even as she reached adulthood and decided to become a courtesan like the women around her.

"Oh, Lucius, your cock is so *large!*" Rozlyn squealed, riding her patron to the utmost bliss. He lay below her, his pale, soft body drenched in sweat. "I'm coming." She moaned her second fake orgasm.

"Fuck me harder. Clench those legs tighter. Roll those beautiful hips," Lucius begged, his fingers awkwardly digging into her flesh as she gave the performance of her life. Then a deep and heavy grunt left his thin, parted lips.

Rozlyn's chest heaved, her large breasts in Lucius's callused hands. Once he caught his breath, she leaned to the side and collected a dry rag from the bedside table. She dabbed the fabric against his damp brow, his reddened cheeks, and neck. Lucius frequented the brothel every week, always requesting her, and always paying double the coin, more than she believed she deserved.

"That was absolute perfection, Rozlyn," Lucius rasped. "I'll always come to you until my dying breath."

Lucius wasn't the most attractive man, but he was kind and worthy of finding someone who he would never have to pay a single coin to bed. "You deserve true love." She bopped him on the nose with a smile. "But you're my favorite patron. I'm not telling you that because you pay me either—you genuinely are."

He ran his fingers through her long hair, the corners of his lips turning downward. "This is the closest I've come to finding love."

"You'll discover her one day," she promised. "Now, you need to go before you're late to work, and I must get ready!" With a quick kiss to his lips, she lifted off him and plucked another rag to clean herself. Her golden locks brushed the floor as she slipped on a silk robe. She ran her fingers over the little white doves she'd sewn into the buttery-hued fabric with care—the perfect robe for any patron to remove before pleasure.

As Lucius drew on his tunic and trousers, Rozlyn took a swig of the bitter tonic to prevent any chance of pregnancy. A child wasn't something she wanted any time soon, but she would enjoy making clothing for anyone else's. For years she wished for a dress shop, and one day, she hoped to save enough coin to no longer chase her dream, but catch it.

Lucius fished three extra coins from his pocket and placed them on the bedside table. "See you soon, Rozlyn."

She gave him a tight hug. "You too, handsome."

After Lucius pushed the scarlet curtains aside and left, Rozlyn scampered to the bathing chamber to prepare for a potential afternoon client. Oscar, a frequent patron, would be selecting one of the courtesans to accompany him on a work journey to the northernmost part of the court.

The chamber was empty, the other courtesans most likely already applying their powders and rouge in their rooms to look their finest. Rozlyn filled one of the four baths, then washed herself with a vanilla soap bar as she hummed a cheerful melody. She scrubbed away every last lingering scent of pleasure before hurrying to prepare herself.

Once Rozlyn finished and returned to her room, she towel-dried her ankle-length hair the best she could. All of the courtesans grew their hair to please the gentlemen who would pay them a visit. It was the signature style of the brothels in Grimm's Dawnbreak Court, a testament to their womanly beauty. Even though Madam hadn't forced Rozlyn to work at the brothel, she'd encouraged her to keep her hair long at an early age, to show that femininity was a strength.

The dress Rozlyn chose for the selection was one of yellow chiffon and muslin, the sleeves sheer, and stitched with tiny pink flowers throughout. She examined her reflection in the oval mirror—soft rose powders accentuated her chestnut eyes and cheekbones, the pink rouge making her lips appear plumper.

"Rozlyn!" her friend Cordelia, and fellow courtesan, called through the curtains. "Madam is growing impatient."

"Oh, sorry!" She set the rouge down and combed through her damp locks to find Cordelia as pretty as a perky daisy out in the hallway. "You wore the dress I made!"

"Of course. It's beautiful." Cordelia grinned, trailing her fingers over the lacy bodice of the royal blue garment. "Now, come on!"

Barefoot, Rozlyn padded across the wooden floor to meet with the other nine courtesans, who stood before thick velvet curtains in the sitting room, their long hair hanging freely. The familiar scent of lavender and honey was bolder here than in the rest of the brothel.

Gray plaits framed Madam's oval face, and fine lines gave prominence to her deep brown eyes. She cast Rozlyn a disapproving stare, but then smiled her welcoming smile. "Be quicker next time," she chided.

"I will," Rozlyn vowed, taking her place between Cordelia and a gorgeous brunette named Trysta. No matter how much she tried, Rozlyn was always late, but she always did her best when it really mattered.

The drapes were drawn shut, and candlelight flickered in the room, casting shadows to set the mood and give the allure of pleasure to come.

A few moments later, the door opened to a tall man ornamented entirely in black. Gloves covered his thin hands, his hood drawn too low to see anything but shadows. Certainly not Oscar, unless he was roaming the streets in disguise so his wife wouldn't hear of his whereabouts. But if he planned to take one of the courtesans with him, she would surely hear of it anyway.

Without a word, the mysterious stranger inched closer to the courtesans, his cloak swept around his bony shoulders. *No, not Oscar*—the older patron was much more built than this scrawny stranger.

"This one might break before our task is done," Cordelia snickered under her breath.

Madam stepped between the man and the courtesans before he could come closer. "How may I help you, good sir?" she asked, a warning in her voice if, without her consent, he got any nearer to what she considered her flowers.

"My name is Iseult," a low voice said. "I am Sorcerer

Marquis Haven Darrow's assistant and am here in his stead. He requests a maiden for a stay in his tower. The length of time is yet to be determined, but both she and you will be handsomely rewarded for her services. *More* than you could imagine. I have the marquis' magical seal, his signature, and his shadows if you don't trust my word." He reached inside his cloak and took out an obsidian envelope, then held it toward Madam.

Furrowing her brow, she broke the wax seal and tiny shadows of snakes swayed along its surface as she opened the paper. "This is indeed from the Marquis of Shadows," Madam announced, turning to the courtesans. "It's the sorcerer's seal and his spelled signature."

The Marquis of Shadows was known as the strongest sorcerer, not only in their court but in all of Grimm. His gothic tower could appear in a single location of any court he wished, yet he hadn't been seen outside his home in two years. It was highly gossiped about that he'd locked himself away inside his tower after his lover chose to wed the lord of the Souldark Court over him. A court where only the dead and sorcerers could enter.

"You're welcome to pick a flower." Madam motioned Iseult toward the courtesans.

The assistant only searched one of the women's faces, then moved instinctually toward Rozlyn and lifted a lock of her long hair. He kneaded the golden strands between his nimble fingers as if he were rubbing a coin for good luck.

"Her," Iseult said, his tone assured. He retrieved a large velvet sack from inside his cloak and opened it to show it was full of shiny silver coins. "This is the brothel's half of the payment."

Rozlyn's heart beat with glee. If that was the brothel's half, that meant she would receive the same amount. This was the opportunity she'd been waiting for—it meant she could finally afford one of the empty shops in the market where she could sell the designs she made.

"Except for her," Madam replied, concern filling her gaze.

Iseult straightened, his shoulders growing rigid. "Only her. The marquis would want no other."

"Please, Madam," Rozlyn begged, clasping her hands. "This could make our dreams come true, a once-in-a-lifetime chance. I'll be fine, and we won't regret it. I promise." Besides that, she was curious to learn more about the cryptic marquis and his shadows.

Madam's lips formed a tight line, but she finally relented. "The flower accepts."

"We leave at once," Iseult told Rozlyn. "Pack your necessities quickly."

Madam nodded for Rozlyn to go and retrieve her things.

Scurrying to her room, Rozlyn grabbed her over-stuffed satchel that she had packed the prior night in case she'd been chosen by Oscar, as all the courtesans were instructed to do. Even though she could be gone longer with the marquis, Rozlyn didn't need much, only sewing supplies, clothing, and the money she had saved to purchase a shop. When that day came, she imagined it to be the perfect place with a room upstairs where she could live.

After shoving on her boots, she placed her bronze dagger, a gift from Madam, at her hip—just in case. Madam had taught her not only how to pleasure a patron but how to defend herself against one. She could sneak out of any hold, easily draw a blade, and remove an eye if needed. Although she would rather not get her hands messy if she could help it.

Taking a leather tie, she quickly plaited her hair, then slipped on her cloak. When she returned to the sitting area, Iseult lingered alone near the door, and the group of courtesans stood around Madam, all waiting for Rozlyn.

"I hope you're not gone too long," Cordelia said and wiped away a few tears streaming down her olive cheeks. "Tell me *everything* when you return. I want to know what the inside of the marquis' tower is like!"

"Don't cry. I won't be gone forever." It could be only a few days for all she knew, but even if it were longer, she would never abandon her found family. "And I promise I will tell you all about it."

She drew each one of the courtesans into a tight hug, saving Madam for last.

"Thank you, Mama." Rozlyn inhaled her comforting cinnamon scent.

"My sweet dandelion." Madam held her tighter. "You are like a daughter to me. If the marquis is savage to you at all, use your dagger on him and come back to us."

Rozlyn tapped the weapon at her waist, her tone hushed. "A knee to the groin and a fatal slash across the throat."

"Followed by a kick to his corpse," Madam finished while lifting a gift. A small sack of cookies. "For the journey. Be careful."

"I will."

"It looks like Oscar finally arrived!" Cordelia called, lowering her bodice and fluffing up her wild dark curls. She then wrinkled her nose. "Hopefully I'm chosen since Cleetus will be here tonight."

Cleetus was a married man who paid extra to verbally degrade his chosen courtesan while they tumbled. But Rozlyn always looked on the bright side when she played the devious little game with him—he orgasmed almost instantly every time.

With a final goodbye, Rozlyn met Iseult at the door and walked out into the bright afternoon light, a smile spreading her cheeks.

"We must hurry," Iseult said, his pace brisk. "The marquis awaits us."

Rozlyn's shorter legs had to take bigger steps to keep up with the man.

They passed the flower shop and meat market, to which she bid them a short farewell. Near the end stood the three empty shops she could soon choose from to make her own, and she smiled. Then they were on the outskirts of the town, the long trail winding toward the mountains, and Iseult veered off it with Rozlyn attempting to keep up.

"Can we walk a little slower?" she panted as they went deeper into the forest. Her feet ached after walking for what felt like hours, the twigs and leaves snapping beneath her boots. "It's just I'm getting thirsty and didn't think to pack water."

"There's no time. The sun will set soon," he rushed out, worry lacing his tone.

A raven screeched at the same time Rozlyn caught sight of the sorcerer's obsidian tower brushing the sky in the distance. Above them, a murder of crows flocked over the roof. She'd wandered by this area on occasion when visiting the neighboring town to buy unique fabrics that she couldn't find in the market nearest the brothel— sometimes the tower was there, and other times it must've been in a different court. Yet when it was here, birds always seemed drawn to the mysterious tower. Especially the black ones.

As she reached the marquis' home, the sounds of the birds grew louder as though nudging her to keep going toward the tower. She peered at the structure's pitch-black stone walls and the dark vines, blooming with onyx orchids and calla lilies, snaking up its length toward a glistening turret.

Squinting, Rozlyn's gaze settled on a single window with the familiar alabaster stone gargoyle mounted beside it. The gargoyle hadn't always been there, but she couldn't recall when it first started appearing. Perhaps a couple of years ago.

The door creaked open, drawing Rozlyn's stare away from the carving.

"Please come inside," Iseult said, his voice calmer than it had been.

Rozlyn stepped through the open door. He closed it behind her and locked it, slipping the key into his trouser pocket. The entrance hall rested in darkness, but a violet glow poured down a curving staircase. The only other entrance was an open cellar door at the end of the foyer.

"You may go upstairs," he stated. "The marquis will meet with you tonight."

"Thank you." Clutching her satchel, Rozlyn ascended the black steps. She passed no other decorations except for dark candles hanging on the walls, their purple flames guiding her way through the tower, its citrusy scent folding around her.

Glistening onyx cloaked everything inside. The candles continued to burn, their wax unmelted. No one in Grimm inherited internal magic. It could only be wielded through objects and potions created by those chosen by the gods. Sorcerers and sorceresses.

Rozlyn climbed up step after step, feeling as though the curving staircase would never end. By the time she reached the top, her thighs ached and her chest heaved. Before her stood *one* black metal door. A tower this high only contained one door? *Strange.* She wondered what was in the cellar then. More rooms?

Rozlyn entered the lavish space lit with candelabras on shelves, and she gasped. Not black at all. The walls were bright canary with ivory suns and colorful flowers hung along the rafters. The canopied bed, covered in lush yellow silk and ivory fur, hugged a corner of the room, and a matching wardrobe sat in the opposite one. A stained-glass bathtub stood on the other side of the room. She opened the massive wardrobe to find it filled with yellow frilly dresses. This was exactly what her dream bedroom would look like—right down to her favorite color—once her dress shop was successful enough to afford fine fabrics for herself anyway.

Two layers of curtains, sheer yellow for prettiness and silver linen beneath to keep out the light, hung open in front of a rectangular window. Setting her satchel on the floor, Rozlyn unlocked the window and pulled the glass inward to poke her head out. Her stomach dipped as she peered down the side of the tower. Someone could easily plummet to their death from this height. A dove took off beside her, and she turned to face the ivory stone gargoyle guarding the tower.

Up close, he was much larger than she imagined, and if he stood, he would be at least a head taller than her. He sat in a crouched position, long horns curving from his head, massive wings sprouting from his back, and a tail curving over a strong thigh. Her gaze shifted upward, finding a harsh scowl, his lips turned downward with sharp teeth protruding. He had pointed ears like an elf from a storybook, a flat nose, and a sharp jaw that could cut glass. His ivory skin and hair looked to be kissed by the moon itself. Overall, he appeared as though he could be a creature of the gods. As curiosity prodded at her, she reached to touch the marble to see if he was cool or warm, when a knock came behind her, and she hurried to shut the window.

She answered the door, expecting to finally meet the marquis, but it was only Iseult, still cloaked in black from head to toe, carrying a food tray.

"I brought you tea and dinner. I'll be in the cellar if you need any assistance at all." He handed her the tray and parted ways with her before she could thank him.

Rozlyn set the tray on the bedside table, then removed her boots and cloak. She unplaited her hair and ran her fingers through the tangled golden locks.

As she waited for the Marquis of Shadows, she drank the delicious honey tea and polished off the savory lamb stew.

Rozlyn pushed up to stand when the room spun and she fell back down on the mattress. She touched her temples as her eyes grew heavy with sleep.

She knew instantly what had occurred—the little weasel had slipped something into her tea.

HAVEN

It was about fucking time he'd found a bastard princess.

Two years. Two *fucking* years Haven had been trapped as a stone gargoyle atop his tower. Day after day, immobile, confined. Even at night when he broke from his stone entrapment, he was a prisoner within the tower's obsidian walls. No sorcery he'd yet tried could break the curse, but he'd finally found the perfect spell.

All he'd needed was the right girl. The tracking spell he'd cast led them to a brothel of all places, which made acquiring her simple. Iseult had taken Haven's letter and a hefty bag of coin that would be impossible to refuse. While trapped in his stone body, he'd watched his assistant lumber toward town—knowing Iseult would bring back the key to his freedom made each second seem like ten.

Haven had fucked himself royally when he'd dabbled in a spell to murder Lord Adham of the Souldark Court, but it was a matter of honor. The asshole had slithered his way into Vivienne's bed. Haven and Vivienne were matched at an early age, and while her sorcery was levels beneath his, she was the only woman who could so easily bring *him* to his knees.

He loathed her at the moment, but somehow still cared despite the torment he endured because of her. It didn't matter that she claimed to have fallen madly in love with Adham, once the time came, she would bend to Haven's will when Souldark became his court. She would crawl on her knees and beg forgiveness for what she'd caused. What she had *ruined*. And then they would continue their betrothal as if nothing had happened.

Two years as a fucking statue. Vivienne owed him her submission. Not only had it been two years since he'd been bound to this piece of shit tower, but two years since he'd *fucked*.

Yet now he would have what he needed, thanks to his creation—Iseult. Unable to leave, Haven had been forced to create his assistant from scattered bones of enemies that had died in the labyrinth below his tower. It had taken much longer to bring him to life than it would've before the spell against Adham went awry, weakening him. Even now, Iseult could only travel so far from

Haven before his body would break apart.

From his perch, still trapped in stone, Haven had watched as the sun inched lower and lower. And then, having only an hour to spare, Iseult approached with the bastard princess. Once she was led inside the tower's walls, the countdown for sunset had begun. The birds circled above him, always attracted to his tower.

The sky darkened, the magic from Haven's onyx thumb ring sending a crackling through him. *Finally*. A soft popping sensation came in the joints of his hands, then spread further. The ball and sockets of his shoulders and knees gave a sickening squelch inside his stone casing as acidic bile rose up his throat.

Thump. Thump-thump. Haven's heartbeat. Blood raced through his dry veins, and his muscles spasmed. The stone fractured along his wings, the deep sound piercing the air. It wouldn't be long now… He tested his limbs, the stone giving slightly. His lungs ached for the breath he'd been denied throughout the day, and he flexed his muscles.

Stone crumbled around him, raining down the side of his dark tower, then vanishing as though it had never existed. A low, satisfied growl rumbled from his chest.

Stretching, Haven broke free from the remaining stone that clung to his alabaster flesh. He shook the dust from his hair, pulling tangled white strands away from his horns, and worked his wings. He wouldn't need to suffer much longer. Once he bound himself to the pathetic princess who so willingly came to his tower, things would change.

Behind him, his assistant had already opened the window. Haven bent, grabbing the edge of the roof and swung inside in one movement, landing on his bare, clawed feet. Right into the most obnoxious bedchamber he'd ever seen.

Yellow walls, yellow rugs, yellow bedding. His lips curled in distaste. The room was meant to relax the bastard princess when she arrived, morphing into whatever she desired most so she would be more trusting.

Still wearing his cloak and gloves, Iseult waited for Haven beside the window with a silver flask. Haven took the liquor and downed it, relishing the burn.

His gaze snapped to Iseult. "You can remove your hood now."

Haven's assistant obeyed and brought the black velvet back to reveal an alabaster skull, dark shadows swirling in the depths of his sockets.

Haven prowled toward the bed where the golden-haired maiden slumbered atop the blankets. Long locks rested beside her in a messy pile. Yellow fabric with hand-embroidered pink flowers covered her curvy form. Her chest rose and fell, giving him a glimpse of her cleavage where the top hung low. His gaze trailed up from her chest to her face. An upturned nose, low cheekbones, long lashes, light pink lips, freckles dusting her cheeks and nose. *Decently attractive.* But nothing compared to

Vivienne.

"I found her at the brothel like you said," Iseult told him. "She's a courtesan."

Furrowing his brow, he slowly turned to face his assistant. When the spell had located her at the brothel, Haven assumed they were simply hiding her. Or making her scrub floors. "A courtesan? Are you sure she's even a princess?" Bastard or not, princesses weren't a part of the skin trade. Hot blood churned within his veins, and he swore to the gods that if this was just an ordinary maiden, he would break his assistant apart.

"The magic stone you gave me warmed in my hand when I touched her hair. Unless I imagined it…"

Haven's nostrils flared. "You better pray you didn't."

"She will wake any moment, Marquis." There wasn't an ounce of fear in his assistant's voice, only acceptance. "I put just enough sleep aid in her tea to make certain she didn't cause any trouble when you came into the room."

A small, pitiful sigh escaped the girl. Her eyelids fluttered open, her head lolling to the side. As her gaze found Haven's, an ear-piercing shriek escaped her lips, then rose another octave when she focused on Iseult's skeletal face.

The maiden snatched a dagger from her waist and leapt into a crouched position on top of the mattress. "Who are you?" she demanded.

Haven caught his gargoyle reflection in the mirror and cursed himself. He hadn't thought she'd wake quite yet, giving him a few minutes to look more *acceptable* so she wouldn't react like … well, *this*. He rolled his shoulders, pulling in the creature until he appeared human before her. He'd created the shifting ability along with his shadows at four years old, and the spell had drained the color from his black hair and brown eyes. But at least he no longer had horns, wings, and a tail.

He waved a hand in the air and shadows curled out from his body, cocooning him, until a black tunic, trousers, and boots covered his body. Most shifters flaunted their nudity, but he preferred to save that for when he used to fuck Vivienne. Besides, shifters couldn't spell clothing any time they wanted—he could.

"Apologies, maiden," he said. "I'm Marquis Haven Darrow. And you've already met my assistant Iseult. Forgive the sleep aid—I didn't want you running off if you saw me come through the window."

"So, you're…" The maiden paused, studying him. "I should've recognized those horns from the gargoyle outside." She angled her head, her shoulders relaxing. "He's a skeleton."

"You noticed," Haven mumbled. She didn't seem to be the brightest, but that didn't make any difference.

"You're not only a sorcerer with shadows but a gargoyle shifter?"

"How wonderful that you've got a pair of eyes." It was his best attempt at appearing gentlemanly. "And your name?"

"Rozlyn," she replied with a bright smile and tucked the dagger back at her waist.

"Rozlyn." Haven took a deep swallow to force out the next words. "My fair maiden, should we celebrate?"

He backed away from the bed and snapped his fingers. A yellow partition broke through the walls and divided the room into two. *Hideous*, he growled inside his head.

"Celebrate?" Rozlyn chirped through the partition. "What are we celebrating?"

"That I'm free now. You broke my curse when you came here," Haven lied, sweetening his tone. "I was foolish and clumsily put the wrong ingredients into a spell which is why no court has seen me in two years, and now I'm free. So pick a gown from your wardrobe, and we'll have a merry ol' time." He rolled his eyes at the nonsense coming from his mouth.

"Oh, how wonderful!" she called, and he could hear her practically beaming with anticipation. "Of course, I'll pick a dress and prepare myself."

The swishing of fabrics sounded as she sifted through them just after another door shut, signaling Iseult leaving.

Haven cranked the lever of the stained-glass tub once, triggering the spell, and it filled with scented water. He sniffed the air and frowned. It smelled of dew-covered grass on a crisp spring day. Even the stained-glass tub depicted a garden of white and yellow tulips.

He grunted his displeasure at being in this pitiful room

for even a minute. The ceremony would begin soon, and that only made his scowl deepen. *This is simply the way to get Vivienne to be mine again*, he reminded himself.

As the bath filled, he snapped his fingers and a plate of pork and vegetables appeared from the kitchen below the tower. He wolfed the meal down until his appetite was sated, then he flicked a hand in the air, making his clothing vanish before stepping into the hot water. The tub was one of the daintiest things he'd ever seen, and as he leaned back, Haven half expected the glass to shatter around him.

"Fuck," Haven ground out as the water soothed his sore muscles. After holding the same position all day while stuck as stone, his body always ached.

A rustling of silks echoed as Rozlyn must've slipped a dress on. It only reminded him of how badly he wanted to fuck his match again. While he thought about Vivienne's lithe body, her perky breasts, the taste of her sweet pussy, his cock stiffened.

The hot water lapped gently up his abdomen, caressing him, intensifying his arousal. Haven couldn't be patient at the ceremony in this manner, so he called out one of his shadows to grip his hard length, making him groan. He didn't give a fuck if the maiden was on the other side of the partition and could hear him, as long as he was away from prying eyes.

When the swells of Rozlyn's large breasts came to mind, he begrudgingly shoved the image from his thoughts and focused again on Vivienne. The way his teeth would graze her pebbled nipple while his fingers circled her swollen clit. How he would taste up her neck, biting into her soft flesh and wrapping a fist around her silky black hair while he buried himself inside her tight cunt.

With one stroke of his shadow, Haven's body responded eagerly, the tip of his cock rose just above the water. There was no time to waste drawing out the pleasure—he needed to come and get on with the binding. His shadow worked furiously, dragging him swiftly toward climax. Water sloshed up his chest and splashed over the sides of the tub. He squeezed his eyes shut, his shadow moving faster.

Haven imagined Rozlyn's expression when she discovered what was to come soon enough. Would she be shocked? Scream? Threaten him? Or none of those since she was here for coin?

He wondered how many men she'd fucked at the brothel, how many times she truly had an orgasm, how hard she rode a patron to gratification.

Fuck. Stop thinking about her.

Haven focused on Vivienne's hand around his cock, then forced himself to just *feel*. Within moments, warm cum spilled across his abdomen, and his body relaxed into the glass tub, his breath ragged. The climax had been rough and forced, but at least he'd be able to focus on the important part of the evening now.

Once his shadow slipped back inside him, he sunk deeper into the water and rinsed his stomach. Letting the warmth soak into his stiff joints, Haven lingered in the bath for a few moments before he finished cleaning himself.

After drying quickly with a fluffy yellow towel, he snapped his fingers, redressing once more.

"Are you presentable?" Haven asked, squeezing the moisture from his hair.

"Yes!" Rozlyn chirped.

He motioned for the partition to sink back into the wall, and when his gaze met Rozlyn, he stilled.

"What the *fuck* are you wearing?" he asked without ushering an ounce of sweetness into his words. Rozlyn's wavy golden hair hung to her ankles, and she wore a tulle-infested, poofy yellow dress with far too many sequins. The only thing redeemable about it was the square, low-cut neckline that displayed the swells of her large breasts.

"Should I choose another?" Rozlyn didn't seem the least bit fazed and glanced toward the open wardrobe, where *every* gown appeared just as gaudy. And fucking *yellow*. Ruffles, lace, ribbons. All *poofy*. Who the hell was this woman?

"No, it's … perfect." Haven forced a smile. "Stay here for a moment while I speak with Iseult."

ROZLYN

Rozlyn glided her hands down the front of her gorgeous gown, the sequins and tulle tickling her palms. Wondrous dresses filled the wardrobe, ones more elegant than anything she could've imagined owning. Silk. Chiffon. Gossamer. Wool. Velvet. She could still feel their lush and pleasing materials against her fingertips.

Haven had brought Iseult back into the room before speaking to his assistant in a shadowed corner, their voices remaining low. The marquis had attempted to hide his broody demeanor to make her feel at home, but once the celebration ended, she would bed him if he wished and she would make certain he relaxed. She'd heard him pleasure himself through the partition, yet even as he orgasmed, it wasn't a fulfilling sound, not in the least. Maybe he didn't know how to pleasure himself thoroughly?

After it was revealed he'd been under a wretched curse of his own making, she understood his gloomy mood. No one deserved to remain a stone gargoyle trapped outside a tower where birds could leave droppings on them each day. Or perhaps *some* did, depending on their crime.

Still glowering, Haven glanced in her direction and rolled a shirt sleeve to his elbow. As she stepped toward him, he resumed his secret conversation with Iseult, and she moved back into her previous position. A courtesan would remain in place until she was called upon. She hadn't been to many court celebrations, only if a patron paid for her to accompany him, otherwise she'd been busy performing her pleasurable duties at the brothel.

Never had she seen a gargoyle shifter before, nor a walking skeleton—both had to have been created by Haven's sorcery. At first when she'd awoken, she believed she'd died, unknowing if she'd become a spirit and was in the darkened pits of the Souldark Court or in the gods' otherworldly embrace. Once she had gotten a better look at Iseult, she'd found him rather adorable with an oblong skull and a snaggle tooth. He no longer wore his gloves, revealing his thin alabaster bone fingers. However, she was still not happy about him slipping a sleep aid into her tea, but she supposed she understood the reasoning.

When standing in all his bare gargoyle glory, Haven's

flesh had remained white. His fangs sharper, coming to fine points and beautifully monstrous, and his shadows were purely ethereal.

As she studied the marquis' human form now, he looked as though he was sculpted by an artist. Pristine nose, lovely jaw, and she would swear it true to the grave, like a perfect dress, his face was impeccably symmetrical. His brows held a black hue, his hair white and hanging down his back, while dark kohl rimmed his pale blue eyes. He was much taller than her, and he wore his clothing flawlessly tailored around taut muscles. She'd only caught a glimpse of his manhood as the gargoyle—it was a gift that wouldn't make pleasing a woman difficult. Madam could only dream of having a man like him working in her brothel. At least if his cock remained the same in his human form.

"Maiden," Haven said, drawing Rozlyn out of her musings. "It's time for the celebration."

"Will there not be music?" she asked. Violins were always at the village dances while harps and pianos accompanied them at lavish parties or fancy balls.

Haven scowled. "No music."

The type to prefer silence then, and since he was her patron, he would get what he wished. Once she received payment, she would purchase her shop and cling onto these charming memories that got her there.

"Hold out your hand," he continued. "I have a gift for you." Smile widening, Rozlyn lifted her arm, and a bouquet of black roses magically appeared in her grasp. What a dreary man, yet it was the thought that counted and a gift nonetheless. She lifted the bouquet to her nose and inhaled the divine floral scent.

The marquis sauntered toward her until only a small gap was left between them. He hovered above her—an alluring scent of citrus, bolder than the tower, wafted off him. She craned her neck to get a better look at him, and her breath caught at how exquisite his face truly was.

"Iseult wants to say a few words." Haven took the flowers from her and tossed them onto the bed, then clutched both her hands. He held them loosely as if he were shy of a woman's touch. Two years alone in a tower with only a skeleton for a confidant could easily alter a person.

Rozlyn glanced at Iseult as shadows swirled within his sockets, and his jaw parted into what she imagined to be a welcoming smile.

"Close your eyes," Haven instructed. "You'll like the next surprise."

Oh! Rozlyn hurried to shut her eyes, and two warm hands skimmed up her arms before a finger lightly traced her lips. She cracked open an eye to find it wasn't Haven's touch but his shadows'. So he wanted *that* sort of surprise. And with his *shadows*. A pool of heat stirred low in her belly at the thought of how the silhouettes could be used to his advantage if he willed it.

When the shadows slipped beneath her flesh, she

gasped as they tickled her insides, caressing her muscles, nerves, and bones.

And then the sensations ceased.

Iseult cleared his voice and spoke softly, "On this day, Rozlyn and Haven, you are now bound as one."

Rozlyn stilled, her eyes widening. *What did he just say?* "Excuse me," she hissed. "What do you mean *bound* as one?" That was a term used typically at weddings. This was a celebration of his freedom.

"It had to be done, maiden," Haven said, a deceitful smile in his tone. "We had to be wed and bound for the curse to fade completely."

"*Married?*" she hissed, jabbing a finger into his chest. "No, no, no, I'm not married to you."

As Rozlyn peered at her surroundings, the room tilted sideways. She was no longer in a yellow sunshine dream, but, instead, a damp, blackened husk of a room.

"You will give me a lock of your hair." Haven lifted his hand, and a shadow curled out from his palm.

Rozlyn leapt backward as the shadow reached for her hair. "No, sir. I won't allow it. Now undo the marriage bond!" Her hair was sacred—all the courtesans' hair was. And even though she was planning to one day own a dress shop, she would always be a courtesan at heart.

As the shadow slinked toward her again, she dodged the devious thing and wound her hair around her arm. *Deep red hair.*

"What did you do to me?" Rozlyn shrieked while

staring in horror at her locks that were no longer golden, but the shade of *blood*. On her opposite wrist, an obsidian marble cuff circled her flesh, and the dress she wore was now a dark gothic frock with black lace, sheer sleeves, and a silken skirt. The only familiar thing that remained was the square neckline.

"It's an improvement," Haven grunted. "The marriage won't last forever, but I do require a lock of hair. Now."

Her stare flicked to an ornate oval mirror, and she nearly fainted at her reflection. Black rouge stained her lips, dark powders circled her eyes, and glittering gray shadow highlighted her pale cheekbones. She could've been the twin sister of a corpse.

"If this is how you want me to dress as your courtesan, then I will. But my hair is off the table." Her tone vowed no room for argument.

Haven's gaze turned slitted. "I know you will, *princess*, but you're no longer a courtesan. You're my wife." He lifted his arm where a matching cuff wrapped around his left wrist.

Rozlyn's heart thundered, and she felt the blood drain from her face. "Why would you call me a princess? I'm nothing of the sort."

He tsked. "My apologies. Does *bastard princess* suit you better? And before you deny it, the binding spell wouldn't have worked if it weren't true."

How did the marquis know about her true parentage?

It was a secret only she and Madam knew. Rozlyn held her tongue, otherwise she would spew the foulest of language that she'd only used for patrons who paid her for it.

"No retorts?" Haven asked. "Brilliant. Don't worry, you'll be paid handsomely for the length of time you're here."

She pursed her lips. Payment for how long though? The bag of coins Iseult gave Madam wasn't nearly enough for something like this.

"Leave, Iseult," Haven continued. Once his assistant slipped from the room, he focused on Rozlyn, his voice curious. "Why are you working in a brothel when you're an heir to the Dawnbreak throne?"

She knew that the king of her court had daughters younger than her, which didn't make Rozlyn just an heir, but *the* heir. Not once had she ever met the princesses, but it didn't matter—from what she'd heard, the eldest daughter would one day make a wonderful queen, and the youngest was just as kind as her older sister. There was no need for Rozlyn to intervene—she wanted to choose her own path, not have it predestined for her.

Coming forward for the crown now would only start a war. Rozlyn's mother had abandoned her years ago and Madam found her and took her in. She'd left it up to Rozlyn to decide whether she wanted to stay at the brothel or be taken to the king. Rozlyn had chosen to remain with Madam and never once regretted the decision.

"I don't consider myself a princess in the least. I'm a courtesan. A seamstress. A woman of the Dawnbreak Court. That's what I am." Rozlyn pulled back her shoulders and stood proudly.

He arched a brow. "You lack any real ambition."

She placed her hands on her hips. "You shouldn't have lied to me. If you'd only told me that you needed to wed to break the curse, I—"

"Would've left," he cut her off. "Even if you had stayed to hear me out, I have no real time frame for how long I'll need you. Don't pretend you would've agreed."

That part was probably true, if it was years and years. But she wouldn't have just allowed him to suffer through a curse—she would've tried to seek aid for the marquis.

"And what about this new jewelry I have?" Rozlyn tapped at her wrist cuff. "Does it need to remain on me this *unknown* length of time too?" When Haven only studied her with a neutral expression, she waved her hand in front of his face. "Hello, can you hear me? Or are you a statue again? Perhaps there is stone blocking your ears?"

"At the moment I wish there was," he mumbled. "Once the curse fades completely, the cuff will disappear. Until then, you'll remain here as my *wife*. Now, give me a lock of hair or the curse will return. Then you'll be trapped in this tower until the day you die."

Rozlyn's heart lodged in her throat. *Forever.* She squeezed her hair as a life living in the tower flashed before her eyes. Her, withered and gray, peering out the window of this room and on the brink of death without ever opening her dress shop.

She finally relented after that horrific thought. "Fine. One *tiny* lock."

His shadow weaved toward her, two blades like scissors shaping, and sliced through the ends she held up. The small tendril fell into Haven's awaiting palm. "There, that wasn't so bad," he said as he tucked the hair into a sable hexagonal locket around his neck.

No matter the length, Rozlyn mourned the loss of her hair, but not for long. Her eyes widened in disbelief as the tiny portion grew back, and a sigh of relief escaped her.

If it were to be a proper marriage with the Marquis of Shadows, she knew what came after a wedding. Pulling back her shoulders, she straightened her spine as she'd been taught to do in this circumstance. "A wife pleasures a husband—a courtesan satisfies her patron."

"What are you talking about, maiden?" Haven asked.

Rozlyn's fingers brushed the velvet buttons lining the front of her frock and loosened the first two. As she reached the third one to reveal her breasts, Haven snatched her hands away from the fabric. His face turned stony, his expression hard.

"We're not fucking," he ground out. "Occupy yourself with something else."

Hmm. Rozlyn stared wide-eyed, baffled by his response. Yet, to receive payment for not having to pleasure someone for once? It was an interesting turn of events.

"Of course," Rozlyn said. While taking in the room, the only colorful items remaining were her satchel and the dress and cloak she'd worn earlier that were now pooled beside the wardrobe. "I'll redesign my dress unless you change your mind." She collected the fabric and sat on the floor. As she fished out sewing supplies from her satchel, Haven's shadow fell over her.

"Did you"—the marquis motioned at the fabric with a finger—"make that?"

"Yes." She sighed blissfully, running her hands down the front of her flowered dress.

"Mmm, that's rather unfortunate."

Rozlyn blinked at him several times. "Well, it's rather unfortunate you believe that." She shrugged, then unraveled her spool of thread.

Without another word, Haven's body writhed, his tunic and boots vanishing, leaving only his trousers behind. Wings emerged from the marquis' back and a tail pierced through his trousers. Haven's skin lightened to stark white, his facial features changing shape until he took the form of his gargoyle.

"This better fucking work," he growled, then slipped out the window and leapt off the edge.

Rozlyn squeaked and rushed to the open space to find the gargoyle safely flying into the night. He'd escaped the tower, so perhaps she wouldn't be here too long after all.

But *here* wasn't what she expected at all.

The tower was no longer in Dawnbreak.

A light mist swayed against a desolate landscape, the surrounding trees gray in color—not a single leaf on any of their limbs. The stars and moon were the only pleasant things out there, but even their shine appeared dimmer than usual.

In the distance, soft and deep moans drifted through the air. Besides the dead, only ones who held sorcery could enter this grim court, and she had nothing of that sort. She was nothing but a bastard princess and a courtesan.

Rozlyn peered down at the marble cuff ensnaring her wrist, reminding her that she was bound to the Marquis of Shadows, the one sorcerer who could find a way to alter rules.

And so, she'd entered the Souldark Court.

HAVEN

The strong scent of burning wood struck Haven's nostrils as he cracked his wings against the harsh wind. This was one of the more bearable sides of the Souldark Court he'd traveled through. Near the lord's castle pine permeated the air, but he wouldn't risk going there just yet. Further north, rot and sulfur wafted from the murky swamps. Even now, he could smell that vile, acrid stench.

Mist-like rain pelted his face as the wind blew harder. He frowned up at the stormy sky riddled with bright stars. Every night for the past two years, he'd wanted to rip them all from the sky and scatter them to the ground. The gods had probably been studying him as he was stuck in his tower, laughing about how pathetic of a sorcerer he'd been. Haven was once the greatest in all of Grimm and he'd still managed to curse himself in the most pathetic of ways. But that was all about to change. He would show the gods how powerful he was by taking the Souldark Court as his own.

The miserable marriage cuff squeezed Haven's wrist, alerting him that there was distance between him and his new wife. Part of him yearned to be at her side, but the logical part knew it was a ramification of being bound. Once the *temporary* binding to the bastard princess removed the entirety of the curse from his blood and bones, he'd be rid of the courtesan and her unbearable brightness.

Below, the mist thinned, and the barren landscape shone beneath the silvery moonlight, mirroring ash, death. Soaring over coagulated marshes, white smoke curled up from their dark surfaces like dozens of tiny clawed hands. Lost gray spirits roamed across the land, and hunched creatures, their horns much longer and wider than Haven's, hid in the shadows to drain energy from the wandering souls.

Fairward, the silver lake where souls would cross over to the After gleamed, the surface rippling. It was the only slice of beauty in this gods damn broken pit of a place. Spirits waited in a winding line near the empty gondola that resumed its repeated voyage at dawn, steered by its residential ferryman, Nightshade.

And Nightshade was precisely who Haven needed to

consult with before paying Adham a long overdue visit. At night, the ferryman usually lingered inside his secluded manor, either fucking spirits or getting drunk on white wine, so he dove down to the land on the barren lawn.

Haven took a swig from his bottomless flask, relieved he wasn't trapped at his forsaken tower. As the liquor burned his throat, he thought again about the bastard princess, and how easily she'd reached for the buttons of her dress, moments away from revealing her lush breasts—so willing to fuck a man who'd ensnared her for his own purposes. For coin. He wondered what else she would do for a price. Perhaps anything he wished...

But he couldn't allow himself to be tempted by her, or any other— his focus was set on reclaiming the woman who the matchmaker had chosen for him. His thoughts turned to how he would kill the Souldark lord and break Vivienne by making her watch. She wouldn't always be heartbroken and miserable over Adham's loss. With enough time, she would desire Haven again and yearn for his touch. He would make her *beg* for it. For him to become her match once more. For the pleasure of his cock filling her.

Nightshade's slate manor loomed tall, its alabaster turrets mirroring a beacon among dead trees and withered stumps. Haven stretched his wings again before he walked across the pebbled ground and drew the appendages into his back. His shadows hid away inside him, but, with a snap of his fingers, his shirt and boots returned.

A dried-up narrow stream and ashy bushes surrounded the perimeter of Nightshade's manor. The floating orange orbs that Haven had spelled for the ferryman years ago glowed brightly to keep the spirits from bothering him when he was home. Nightshade had to shield their eyes when he brought them there to fuck so they didn't begin screeching.

The manor was decent for a ferryman, but for someone who did all the work in such a horrendous court, Haven had to admit that Nightshade deserved more than he'd been given. Which was how he knew he could lure the man to Haven's side—the marquis had already given him more than any lord ever had.

Black curtains draped the tall windows, and a marble statue stood on either side of the front door. The one of the Souldark lord had always been there, but the other— a lady in a long gown—was new. *Vivienne.* The statue matched her lithe figure and facial features perfectly. Haven's nostrils flared, and he released his shadows like whips, slicing through both statues, their bodies cracking and falling in pieces to the ground. A statue would be remade of Vivienne once he was lord, and after *he* said it could be.

Haven didn't bother to knock—he released a thin shadow to lift the latch. Throwing open the door, he barged inside Nightshade's home, where the scent of sex permeated the air. He didn't have to venture far to find the ferryman in the sitting room, fucking a spirit in front of a crackling fireplace. His silver hair hung just past his chin as he rested on his knees and thrust into the pale gray spirit. The woman's breasts bounced, and one of Nightshade's hands was planted on her back, the other at her hip.

The spirit seemed too consumed by pleasure to spare the Marquis of Shadows a glance. Nightshade, on the other hand, met Haven's gaze just before his pitch-black eyes widened in surprise.

"Where *the fuck* have you been?" Nightshade called, his voice gruff as he continued his rhythmic pounding inside the woman's pussy.

The spirit finally looked Haven's way and bit her lip, clearly liking what she saw. Some spirits carried around pent-up lust from years of being alone in Souldark, either unwilling or unable to go into the After. Haven had no interest in fucking dead things though.

"I wanted a bit of solitude," Haven said to the ferryman.

"Let me finish this and we'll talk," Nightshade groaned, his pace growing wilder, his pelvis slapping against the woman's ass until she cried in pleasure.

Haven glowered and folded his arms while waiting for the ferryman to orgasm. He nearly used a shadow to rip Nightshade off the woman, but he would give the bastard a couple more moments since he was the only semi-bearable one in this abysmal court.

Once the ferryman grunted his release, he drew the pleasure out a little longer by pulling the woman's back against his chest and massaging her clit. Her erotic moan filled the room.

"For fuck's sake, Nightshade!" Haven growled.

He smirked at Haven and whispered something into the spirit's ear. She giggled before slipping on her long gown, then Nightshade slapped her ass and purred, "I have more to teach you. *Very* soon."

The woman smiled bashfully at Haven while scurrying past him as though she were a proper lady and he hadn't just witnessed her getting fucked.

Nightshade sat against the wall beside the fireplace and propped his arm on his left knee, his cock in full view.

Haven scowled. "Put on a pair of fucking trousers."

"She clearly wanted you too, and by your attitude, it seems like you might need a cunt." Nightshade grinned as he stood and tugged on his trousers, leaving them unfastened.

Even though Haven towered over most villagers, Nightshade was still taller than him. It wasn't surprising given that he wasn't just a ferryman—he was the child of a god and a mortal woman. When the god's wife discovered he'd had a bastard, she bound Nightshade to Souldark as punishment for her husband's infidelity. Only the Souldark lord could grant him freedom, but none of them ever had. Why would they? They needed him to keep the spirits from overrunning their court.

When Haven remained silent, Nightshade lifted a glass of wine from the table near the settee and took a long sip. "Drink. You look like you need some." He motioned to a second glass that must've been there for the spirit.

"No." Haven drew out his flask and tossed back a few swigs of liquor before getting down to business. "I have a request. You will not deny me, nor will you interfere."

Nightshade arched a brow and sank down on the settee. "Oh, is that so? It doesn't sound like much of a request then." Haven had known the ferryman for over fifteen years, ever since he'd started traveling to the Souldark Court when he was eleven years old. They'd first met when Haven brought protection spells to the ferryman for Fairward Lake at the lord's request. The coin he'd made from selling spells to the majority of the courts had made Haven one of the wealthiest sorcerers in Grimm.

"I know you're Adham's lapdog," Haven started, "but I want to make a bargain with you. One that will give you the power you've always deserved."

Nightshade furrowed his brow and ran a hand across his jaw. "And what kind of bargain would that be?"

"Unless you've changed since I saw you last, I know you're sick as fuck of being the ferryman, of being a slave to that bastard lord, rowing souls across Fairward Lake all day long without any true reward."

"Did you not just see me fucking a beautiful woman?"

Nightshade chuckled. "When night falls, I do what I want. My cock is always satisfied."

"In your home," Haven clarified. "The lord doesn't let you leave this area unless it's to run errands for him. A prison for you in a sense." He paused, squaring his shoulders as his shadows slinked out of him. "If you don't interfere with my visit to Adham's castle, I'll make sure you never row another soul again. As lord of this court, I could unchain you from Souldark and you'd be free to go anywhere you want."

Nightshade reclined against the settee's cushions, his head angling to the side. "You want to murder the lord because your fiancée chose to marry him, am I right?"

Haven narrowed his eyes, and his shadows swirled around his fists, begging to choke the ferryman for speaking about that. "Yes."

"It's been two years, Haven." Nightshade sighed. "Any woman would beg for a sorcerer like you to fuck them. Vivienne isn't worth a revenge plot."

Haven didn't give a damn what the ferryman thought. "Your manor is just as pitiful as this dead court. Your lord hasn't done anything for you or the rest of his subjects, not even with a sorceress at his side. So, are you with me or against me?" His shadows slithered across the floor, barbs spreading while creeping toward Nightshade.

"I need something more than freedom." He smirked, ignoring the shadows and polishing off the remainder of his wine. "Something worthwhile."

The image of Rozlyn's fingers brushing the buttons of her dress came to Haven again, a courtesan who would do anything. "I have something, *someone*, you might enjoy."

"I already have plenty of *someones* to enjoy."

Haven raised a brow. "Someone warm. Someone *alive*."

"Go on," Nightshade purred.

"A courtesan resides in my tower, but not just any courtesan—a bastard princess. She's the direct heir to the Dawnbreak Court. You can have her once I'm finished."

"You have a woman who is a professional at pleasing men *and* one who could make you a king? And you want to trade her to me for *Vivienne*?"

"Do you accept or not?"

Nightshade's grin turned wolfish. "It sounds like the perfect bargain, but why can't I have her now?"

"I still need her to rid myself of a curse." Haven lifted his arm, allowing Nightshade to examine the marriage cuff. "She's the key to fully break it, and when the cuff is gone, the maiden is yours."

Nightshade let out a low whistle. "I thought you said that you were enjoying your solitude." When Haven only frowned, the ferryman held out his wrist toward him. "I accept the bargain. Bind our deal so you can't change your mind. I have trust issues after working with lords over the years."

"I won't go back on my word," he vowed. Rozlyn was

nothing to him, only a means to an end. "But if it makes you feel better, I'll bind our agreement."

Haven edged forward, his ring thrumming with energy. He uttered a low incantation as his shadows crawled up Nightshade's legs, his torso, and down his arm to his left wrist. A single inky hand pierced through the ferryman's flesh, and he winced, his veins bulging. When the shadow drew back, a dark crescent moon with an eye at its center tattooed Nightshade's skin.

"It's done," Haven said, whirling around and trudging to the door.

"You need someone other than Vivienne to wet your cock," the ferryman called at his back. "Perhaps you should taste the courtesan before she's mine."

"Fuck you," Haven seethed without sparing him a glance and slipped out into the night. He unfurled his wings, preparing to make the long journey toward the castle. Haven wouldn't perform a spell to toy with Adham at first, he would instead have his shadows rip the bastard's heart out.

He leapt into the sky, with only one thought in his mind. *Kill Adham.* Lightning cracked and thunder rumbled, but the storm never found him. After flying for fucking hours, the sun rose, the first dawn he would have in two years without turning to stone.

A small smile crept over his lips as the morning's rays caressed his skin. *Warm.* He'd almost forgotten how it felt. Then, just as he flew over a pea-colored swamp—the stench of sulfur invading his nose—a blinding white light flashed before his eyes.

A moment later, his vision cleared. But he was no longer crossing over the revolting swamp.

Haven was back inside his fucking tower.

ROZLYN

"Why the fuck am I back in the tower?" Haven growled.

Rozlyn glanced over her shoulder to where the marquis stood pacing near the window, his leather wings tightened at his back, his shadows storming around him like wild flames. He hadn't made a single peep when he came inside the room—it was as though he'd appeared out of thin air.

She set down the dress she'd been stitching and unstitching for most of the night, unable to concentrate on the fabric nor get a wink of sleep. Not after the Marquis of Shadows hadn't warned her that his tower would be traveling to the Souldark Court. She'd known

Haven could make his home disappear from Dawnbreak and place it in any of the other eleven courts, but she hadn't thought that he would bring her to the court that was meant for mostly the dead.

"I don't know. You tell me," Rozlyn finally said. "And while you're at it, you could've at least informed me that we would be traveling to the Souldark Court. Perhaps I could've prepared myself a little more." At first she'd thought she might be dead, but her heart still beat.

Haven halted his pacing, his hard gaze boring into hers. "It's none of your concern where we travel. All you have to do is stay put inside the tower."

"None of my concern?" She blinked, squaring her shoulders. "I could hear the dead moaning and groaning outside all throughout the night!"

Haven rolled his eyes. "Be satisfied they can't come inside my home, maiden."

"And *you* be satisfied that you're no longer a stone gargoyle since it's now day and all," she huffed.

Haven ignored her, then looked out the window, the morning sunlight seeping into the room. His body stilled, and he stood there for what felt like centuries, until she thought he might've become a stone gargoyle once more. But then he slammed a fist against the stone wall while bellowing, "Fuck! Fuck, fuck!"

Rozlyn pushed up from her position on the floor and smoothed the creases of her *gifted* dress. "I do believe if you had a good one of those you might respond to situations in a much calmer manner."

Haven whirled around, his expression stonier than she'd seen it thus far. "Do you think an *orgasm* will solve this damn predicament?" he snapped.

Rozlyn covered her mouth to hide her smile. "Are you certain there isn't at least *some* stone debris left in your ears? I said a *good* one. As a courtesan, we don't generally touch ourselves intimately unless we are learning the way of an orgasm. Sharing pleasure with another is the key to receiving the utmost elation. I might also add, it should be with someone who knows how to perform, not just anyone. A perfect euphoric release can always be taught. I have loosened many men who needed an extra hand."

Haven's lips parted briefly before he pursed them into the tightest of lines. He might not want to admit it, but it was quite obvious he desperately needed a woman's touch.

"If you would like my hand, mouth, or heat around your cock, I'll willingly oblige." Rozlyn perked up like a flower under sunlight as a courtesan always did when offering herself, no matter that he'd lied, trapped her into a marriage, and to all the gods, the worst possible thing, regardless that it had grown back … cut a lock of her *hair*! But she tamped down her annoyance because, for coin toward her future, she would work her damnedest to awaken all of his inner desires. Ride him until his frown turned in the opposite direction.

"I don't need a fuck right now," Haven ground out,

prowling toward her until he hovered above her, his warm breath mingling with hers. The pleasant scent of citrus wafted off him. "But if I did, it wouldn't be with you. I have only one match."

Realization at his words washed over her. "Ah, I see. You're wounded by a woman of your past." Rozlyn nodded, mulling over how his lover had chosen to wed the Lord of Souldark over him. "I've seen this time and time again."

"Shut your mouth, maiden," he hissed.

"Don't you mean *wife*?" she drawled.

"*Wife*"—sarcasm laced his tone—"why don't you look out the window and see what you've done."

"Promise not to throw me out, and I'll peek," she sang with a smile. When his stony expression didn't alter in the least, clearly not in the mood for jests, she went to the window and peered out at the lush green foliage, a flock of black doves flying through the bright blue sky.

They were no longer in Souldark but back in Dawnbreak! *Thank the gods*!

"*I* didn't bring us back here. You or your tower did." Rozlyn glanced over her shoulder at Haven, who stood directly behind her, his chest nearly brushing her back.

"Step aside." Haven grasped her arm and drew her away from the window, neither gently nor harshly.

Haven released her and flexed his fingers at his sides. His wings cracked once, creating a gust of wind within the room, her hair fluttering around her. He then tightened them at his back, slipped out the window to the ledge, and leapt off the tower. Another blast of wind, not from Haven, shoved him back inside the room. With a clenched jaw, he pumped his wings, fighting poorly against the wind, and landed on his back, right at Rozlyn's bare feet.

She tsked, staring down at his pouty lips and miserable face. "Hmm, it looks as though my hair didn't fully help your curse, did it?"

"That's quite obvious," Haven grumbled before getting off the floor and opening his locket. No longer was the tendril a deep shade of blood red but her natural gold. He flung the hair beside her small toe like a petulant child, then held out his hand, a shadow curling out of his palm toward her. "I require another lock of your hair."

Rozlyn thought about telling him no at first, but she remembered how he'd said the curse could return fully, and she'd be trapped in the tower until she died. *No, that would not do.* "How many more tendrils are you going to need?"

"That all depends."

Her chest tightened when she thought about how that *depends* could add up to endless amounts until she was eventually bald. But if each one grew back as they had before, then she could just forget her hair had been cut at all.

"Fine, but you'll owe me," she relented and lifted a small portion of her hair.

He arched a brow at her, and she scooted her fingers back a smidge so the lock would be a little bigger for him. The shadow swirled forward, shaping into scissors, and sliced like knives through butter, the tendril falling into Haven's awaiting palm. Her hair grew back as he snapped his metal locket shut.

Haven stepped over the calamity of a dress she'd been working on and returned to the ledge outside the window, leaping off it as he'd just done moments ago. A loud gust of wind blew against him, his wings cracking like thunder. Yet his fight wasn't enough—the wind hurled him back through the window, and like a recurring dream, he was at her feet once more. Or perhaps not a dream but a nightmare for the Marquis of Shadows.

"For your sake," he said, his pale blue eyes piercing hers, "my tower better not lock me in tonight."

"Did you even think to go downstairs and try the front entrance?" Rozlyn asked. Though it might make more sense for him to take flight from this height, less work, but if he could simply walk out the front door...

Haven's shadows swirled around his muscular torso as his wings tucked inside his back. His ivory skin returned to a sun-kissed glow, his nose elongating to perfection, his tail disappearing, until there was no sign of the gargoyle at all.

As he snapped, his shirt and boots returned, and she had to admit, she was a little disappointed by that.

"Follow me," Haven cooed, and the edges of his lips

curled up. He opened the door, his feet already echoing down the staircase.

Rozlyn clutched her skirts and scurried after the marquis. Even when she reached him, he was more trouble to keep up with than Iseult had been. He stayed stoic and silent while growing interest churned within her. Why would she need to come with him? Would he allow her to accompany him out of the tower if he could leave? Perhaps she could sweeten him up so that she could pick up a few fabrics from the nearest shop to keep her occupied.

At the bottom of the stairs, Haven released a shadow, the inky silhouette forming into the shape of the key similar to the one Iseult had used. It curled toward the lock and turned into smoke. More of his shadows seeped out, clawing at the door, another shaping into an axe and slamming down against it—all morphing into smoke.

Not a sound. Not a budge.

As Haven's shadows slinked back inside him, Rozlyn said, "Iseult used a key to open the door when we first came—you could try that."

Haven smirked. "My shadows are more precise than any key. Apparently, this part of the curse isn't lifted, which means the door remains sealed during the day. And while Iseult may have come in through this door, he didn't go out of it. He dropped from the tower window—sorcery put him back together."

Nausea bubbled in her stomach as she thought about

the sheer drop from that height. Not only the fall, but that this meant she was trapped inside during the day too. Sorcery wouldn't put her back together if she plummeted to the ground. "Hmm."

"There is one other way out of the tower, and that is only for my enemies. I wouldn't suggest becoming one of those—they never quite seem to make it to the exit." Haven's gaze lit up with amusement as he studied her just before he stepped toward the open cellar and descended the winding staircase.

Rozlyn had never once had an enemy. Not with her mother, who'd abandoned her, and not with her king father, who hadn't cared enough to say a simple hello to her when she was younger.

She padded down the second winding staircase and caught up with Haven. This set of stairs was a much shorter distance, the sconces lining the walls holding green flames instead of violet. They entered a large rectangular hallway holding a total of seven doors. Three on her left, three on her right, and one before her, with black cloaking everything except for the flames.

"Since you haven't been given a proper tour, my bedroom and guest bedrooms." Haven gestured to the right. Then he waved to the left. "Kitchen, spell room, spare bathing chamber." He came to a final stop in front of the door at the end of the hallway and rapped the metal lightly with his knuckles. "This room holds an entertaining little labyrinth."

Rozlyn cocked her head as she observed the closed door. "A deadly maze, I take it?" If it was that easy to bypass, his "enemies" would've made it out alive. Unless they were just terrible at labyrinths since their paths could be tricky.

"Very much so." Haven's fingers brushed the onyx handle and he drew the door inward, its hinges creaking slightly.

Thick silver and golden smoke weaved in snakelike patterns, casting a beautiful glow into the hallway. She squinted, straining her eyes to see anything past the barrier, but she couldn't witness a thing. As Rozlyn inched toward the smoke, Haven yanked her by the shoulder, her back smacking into his firm chest.

"Are you a fool?" he asked between gritted teeth.

"I wasn't going to walk inside," Rozlyn said. "I only want to have a peek past the smoke is all."

"Yes, take a peek and become a shriveled husk so you ruin us both," he ground out, taking his hand from her.

Rozlyn's eyes widened. She'd been moments from walking through the smoke, and it killing her? She *did not* want to die today, or any time soon for that matter. "That doesn't seem like a fair obstacle for your opponents."

"Do you think I should give a fuck?" Haven folded his arms and tilted his head to the side.

That would all depend on what his enemies did. "Are *you* able to go through it?" she inquired instead.

"Of course I can, but leaving during daylight hours

still isn't an option for me now. Once night falls, we'll return to *Souldark*." The last word came out desperate. Since he wasn't a spirit, there was only one reason she could think of as to why he sounded so urgent to go back to such a broken place.

"Is this because of the lord and your old lover? The Lady of Souldark?" Rozlyn kept her voice soft, gentle.

"Do not"—Haven paused, his nostrils flaring—"mention either one of them again, maiden." He turned his back on her and bounded up the staircase, his heavy footsteps echoing.

Rozlyn believed it was too soon to go after him, and if he'd wanted her to follow, he would've told her so. That much about the Marquis of Shadows she could already decipher. Though she'd never been in love, she wondered what she would've done if she'd been in his place. A sorcerer could brew a tonic to forget a lover, but that wasn't a choice Rozlyn would make. Sew an entire wardrobe of new dresses to occupy her mind? That seemed more likely.

The door nearest the labyrinth opened, and Iseult stepped into the hallway. "It's good to have another in this tower. Marquis needs the company."

"I'm not sure he *wants* the company. But what about you? Do you like it here?" Rozlyn yawned, exhaustion sweeping over her after a long night.

"Yes, very much. I would work for no one else other than Marquis. Unless he required it, that is." Iseult pointed toward the middle bedroom door. "It's a long walk up the stairs, and you look tired. You may retire in the guest room, and if you want something other than fruit, an abundance of soups and desserts linger in the kitchen due to the Marquis' spells. Nothing else has a sleeping aid, I vow it."

"I should hope not." She winked and entered the guest room since it was much closer. The color theme didn't surprise her—black with a sprinkle of silver and red here and there. Near the back of the room, across from a vanity, rested a large canopied bed, where furred blankets and a collection of silken pillows decorated it. A massive wardrobe hugged the farthest corner, its handles a glistening ruby.

Rozlyn lifted a pear from a glass bowl atop the night table. She stepped out into the hallway to ask Iseult if she should stay in the room after she awoke or wait for the marquis to retrieve her, but he was no longer there. Lifting her fist, she knocked on his door, yet he didn't answer.

Taking a bite of the pear, she stared at the smoke of the labyrinth and considered that the marquis might've deceived her. Perhaps the smoke wasn't dangerous at all and he simply didn't want her to try to escape. Her fingertips squeezed the fruit and she tossed it in.

Sizzling erupted, the smoke's weaving grew faster, and the pear thumped to the floor near her feet, shriveled and black.

Rozlyn slammed the door shut. "I think I'll avoid *that* room forever."

HAVEN

Haven tapped his fingers against the window ledge as he peered out at the Dawnbreak Court. Never had he wished to see a bleak landscape over such lush foliage as he did right then. He needed to see spirits milling about through mist, not crows cawing as they soared past him across the clear sky.

Fuck.

The lord's castle was too far of a journey for him to make after night fell, and while his tower could travel from court to court, there was only one part of Souldark where it appeared—just over the border from Dawnbreak. There was little life in the barren court for his magic to latch onto.

How inconvenient.

His fingers thrummed against the dark stone faster, his nostrils flaring, when the doorknob to the room turned, and he whirled around to tell Rozlyn to leave him alone. But she wasn't the one who'd come after him. Iseult padded in with a tray of sugary pastries, fruits, and a meat pie.

Haven's shoulders fell a fraction. Was that disappointment he felt? Over a woman he was praying hadn't come to apologize for bringing up Adham and Vivienne? *No*, it wasn't. The bastard princess was foolish and grated on his nerves.

"The girl is taking rest in the guest room downstairs," Iseult said, setting the tray on the night table. "I do believe you should eat and do the same. This was your first flight in quite some time. You need your strength, Marquis."

Haven hadn't eaten since before the wedding ceremony, and the savory scent curling up from the meat pie made his stomach growl. He wouldn't admit it, but his assistant had a point. Sinking down on the mattress, he bit into a lush strawberry. "I did everything right with the spell when I bound myself to her. I can feel it," he muttered, the cuff squeezing his wrist, even though Rozlyn was only further down in the tower.

"Perhaps there's more to it," Iseult suggested. "A spell can have many layers. You might need to pull back a few of them first."

Haven shot him a glare. The skeleton had been built

from different bones of the marquis' enemies, and just because some of them had belonged to sorcerers, it didn't make him as knowledgeable as Haven. He could send his assistant out of the tower during the day as he had when he'd collected Rozlyn, but it wouldn't matter unless his home was in Souldark. Even then, the spell would only last for so long once Iseult breached the reach of Haven's sorcery and his bones fell apart. He had no true heart or other organs. And besides that, Haven wanted to be the one who slaughtered the bastard Lord of Souldark.

"Go to the sorcery room and thicken the contents in the large cauldron," he said and motioned Iseult away.

"Yes, Marquis." Iseult bowed his head and softly shut the door behind him.

Haven polished off his meal, the rich lamb inside the meat pie perfectly tender. It tasted just as it would've if he'd gotten meat at the market and cooked it himself. With spells, a good sorcerer could make food appear out of thin air, but a great sorcerer could make it taste finer than any royal meal. Albeit, a *great* sorcerer would never have gotten himself trapped in a fucking curse to begin with.

One damn step at a time.

He would unravel himself from his binds, and his shadows would pave the way.

In the meantime, at least he wasn't a fucking stone gargoyle, forced to endure the birds shitting on him all day. Haven sighed, snapping his fingers for his clothing to vanish so he could bathe before sleeping.

No longer was the tub dainty, nor did the water smell of dew-covered grass on a spring day. Black crystal held the water with a raised swirling design, and evergreen wafted from the liquid. *Perfect.* And yet, as he slipped into the bath, the evergreen didn't soothe him as it usually did… Did he want Rozlyn's chosen scent to return? *No.*

After a quick scrub, Haven relaxed in the water, letting the warmth seep into him. His muscles ached from the long flight that he normally would've had no issue completing, but it had been too long since he'd journeyed that far. Still, it had felt good to release all the pent-up energy that he couldn't get rid of while trapped in the tower.

After he dried himself, simply walking back down the staircase to his bedroom seemed an impossible feat, so he remained where he was. Haven spelled himself a loose pair of trousers and drew back the silk blankets of the bed. He laid down, pressed his head to a feather-soft pillow, and inhaled a welcoming, sunshine scent.

Haven's eyes snapped open and he gazed at the blankets. They were the same as always, a dark shade of midnight and not the bright yellow Rozlyn had slept on, but her scent lingered. A *pleasant* scent that he would never admit he relished. His shadows knew he liked it, but they would keep his secret or fuck off.

With a grunt, he closed his eyes again and drifted further away, collapsing into the same dream he'd witnessed every day for two fucking years.

"I'm sorry, Haven, I can't marry you," Vivienne said, tears beading her long lashes.

"Why?" he asked, his fists shaking. Ever since they were matched by a sorceress matchmaker, he'd wanted no other. She had all the qualities that aligned with his sorcery and made him stronger.

"I never meant for it to happen … to fall in love with Adham," she sobbed, her lower lip wobbling. "I do care about you. So much, Haven, but I'm not in love with you. I know you're not in love with me either. It's the idea of what we could achieve together with sorcery that you truly care about."

"We've been matched since we were children. You couldn't have realized that you didn't love me sooner?" he hissed.

"It's my fault, I know. I'm sorry. I kept trying to love you, I really did. Please forgive me." She reached for him and he pulled away from her touch.

"Leave," Haven said softly. When she didn't move, his shadows slipped from him and he shouted, "Leave me!"

With a hesitant glance back at him, Vivienne shifted into her raven form and flew out his tower window toward the Souldark castle.

Where Adham would soothe her, then fuck her.

It was Haven's fault for introducing Vivienne to the lord, for bringing her to this abysmal court at all, but he'd trusted her, trusted that their matching was unbreakable. If she'd truly cared about Haven, she wouldn't have flown back to the lord so soon, wouldn't have fucked him before calling off their betrothal.

One thing was clear—Adham would die, and Vivienne would

be Haven's once more.

He threw open the door, then pounded down the staircase to the spell room. Death had numerous qualities and could be given in an influx of ways. And Haven knew exactly how he wanted the lord to die. Make Adham's body as still as a statue, unable to move at all. Then he'd send birds to peck his eyes out—black birds with emerald irises so they resembled Vivienne's shifter form. Finally, he would use his shadows to remove Adham's heart while Vivienne watched. She would see that Haven was indeed the most powerful sorcerer, and that he could also break hearts.

Hovering over one of his cauldrons, he hurled in ingredients. "Fuck Adham," he seethed. Haven worked throughout the night until a thin layer of dark smoke curled up from the concoction, tiny birds shaping and unraveling. He couldn't stop, even though he was overworking himself and needed a break, but he was so close.

He rolled his sleeves up and grabbed an empty jar from a shelf. As he moved the glass into the smoke to catch the spell, the emerald-eyed birds spread throughout the room, filling the air, flapping their wings. Haven's shadows clamped down on his shoulders, rooting him firmly in place. A numbness spread up his legs to his torso.

He bellowed an incantation before the smoky birds could turn on him further, pecking out his eyes, just as two of them neared his face. A shadow squeezed his heart, the world stilled, and he froze.

Haven was no longer inside the tower but perched on the roof outside, trapped within stone.

Haven clutched something soft and nuzzled into it, the alluring scent of sunshine calming the angry roar in his veins. "Mmm," he groaned. Such a fucking horrible dream.

"If I knew how nice you could be with a pillow, I would've given you one earlier," a sweet voice interrupted his thoughts.

Haven opened his eyes to find Rozlyn standing before him with a silver flask in her hand. She looked to be freshly clean, her long blood-red hair plaited and damp, a silken black dress hugging her curves flawlessly. The black rouge accentuated her mouth, showing off the perfect bow of her upper lip.

He shoved the pillow to the floor and sat up, running a hand through his mussed hair. "What are you doing here, maiden?"

"Well, the sun is setting soon, so I figured you might want to see if you can get some fresh air again."

The sun was already setting? Haven shot his gaze toward the dark gossamer curtains where barely a sliver of light poured in. He'd slept longer than he'd have liked. *Fuck.* He leapt off the bed and yanked the window open, making sure his sorcery returned the tower to Souldark.

As the sun finally disappeared, the green foliage

outside became a blur, then when the image relaxed, it revealed a barren landscape. Haven sighed in relief while he watched flickering souls in the distance sway across the ground, the mist lighter than the night before. He opened the locket and the tendril remained red.

"Here. Iseult told me this is your favorite. Figured it might lighten your mood." Rozlyn smiled and handed him the flask. When he didn't take it, she added, "There isn't poison in it. But if you really want me to, I could always add a bit of belladonna. Or hemlock might be a better choice."

"I only have oleander in the tower at the moment," Haven grumbled. He took the flask and drank several swigs of liquor. Another tray of food sat at his bedside, this one a plate of salmon and steamed vegetables.

His shirt and boots reappeared with a simple snap of his fingers, his pants changing into a more formal style, and he slid the flask into his pocket. Then he slipped out the window onto the ledge. No wind fought him as he cracked his wings and lifted upward—the night was the same as before. It was possible that being transported back to the tower had been a fluke, but he would see if the following morning would be different. He wouldn't waste energy traveling to the lord's castle tonight for no gods damn reason, so he would wait through the short night. Either the hair would be enough to let him be free, or the magic would snatch him back inside again.

Haven returned inside to find Rozlyn on the floor,

cutting into the fabric of her old dress. He lingered on the edge of the bed to eat his meal while watching her moisten thread between her plump lips and feed it through the eye of a needle.

The marquis chewed his fish, wondering how well she sucked cock, how slow or fast her tongue would lick up his shaft. Not *his*. Nightshade was right about Haven needing to be pleasured … but not by Rozlyn. Vivienne would be the one to give him orgasms.

An idea crossed his mind as he studied Rozlyn's deft movements. "You can sew." A statement, not a question.

"The courtesans say I'm one of the best dressmakers." She beamed and set down her needle.

"People lie all the time." He shoved a few slices of carrots into his mouth and continued to observe the embroidered flower pattern of her dress. Although he would still consider the design unfortunate, it was clear she had real talent.

Rozlyn pursed her lips. "And people lie about you being the greatest sorcerer in Grimm. Considering you managed to trap yourself in your own tower and need my assistance to help reverse it, I might be inclined to disagree."

The edges of his lips tilted up at her boldness. She didn't have a single magical object on her—he could easily squeeze her throat with his shadows, make her beg for mercy. But he needed her.

"Still a spell no others could make." He smirked.

She blinked, her doe eyes latched onto his. He studied her freckles, not noticing before how they were like constellations sprinkled across her cheeks and nose. The courtesan wasn't as tall and lithe as Vivienne, but he couldn't deny she had the breasts of a goddess—at least from the cleavage he could see. He and Vivienne had both been innocent when they'd first went to bed together, and his temporary wife must've fucked countless men, extensively trained in the art of pleasure. The bargain between the marquis and Nightshade had been perfect—the ferryman would be pleased with her.

But … maybe Haven could have a small taste of her first. Just to be sure she was any good, and it would make him and Vivienne even before they reunited. Their gazes still locked on one another, tension filled the air, and he cursed himself for even thinking about being carnal with a courtesan. He stormed out of the room.

"Wait, you seemed like you wanted my assistance!" Rozlyn shouted, her feet pitter-pattering behind him halfway down the staircase.

"I told you we're not fucking," he muttered. It came out more as though he were telling himself instead of the bastard princess.

"No, you made it seem like you wanted me to sew something for you!" she exclaimed.

Haven didn't utter a word until they reached the entrance at the bottom of the tower. That aggravatingly pleasant sunshiny scent of hers washed over him when he turned to face her.

"I want you to make a doll," he said as he thought about reworking the spell that had gone awry. The entertainment would begin before his shadows went in for the kill. He could spell the doll to mirror Adham so that whatever happened to it also occurred to the Lord of Souldark. A concoction would need to be added, and a small incantation spoken to make it effective, but that was easily done.

"A doll?" Rozlyn wrinkled her nose. "I mostly make clothing."

"It's a simple task. Just a vague fabric one. No face or hair. But give him a pompous little suit." One fit for an asshole lord.

"Oh!" She clasped her hands together and smiled. "I can easily do that."

"Wonderful. Go get started." He didn't wait for Rozlyn to scurry away, somehow knowing she would follow him into the spell room instead. Iseult stood at the furthest cauldron in the corner, churning the liquid, the metallic smell clinging to the air.

With eyes like saucers, Rozlyn peered inside the cauldron and tilted her head. "What kind of blood is that?"

"A combination of human and animal." Haven shrugged. "It's how most powerful spells begin. No matter how much you scoop out, this particular cauldron never empties." He rolled up the sleeves of his shirt to get to work when he noticed Rozlyn's gaze trained on his arms. "Yes?" he drawled.

She cleared her throat. "What fabric am I supposed to use?"

"The cabinets behind you should have everything you need." He held up a finger. "Oh, and make the doll small enough to fit in my pocket."

"Of course." She smiled brightly and approached a row of onyx cabinets as if she'd just been given a queen's crown.

His attention focused on Iseult, who continued to stir. "You can leave. Wake me before the sun descends tomorrow."

"Yes, Marquis." Iseult placed the ladle on the hook before leaving Haven and Rozlyn alone.

Throughout the rest of the night, Haven worked on his original spell for Adham while tweaking a few of the ingredients, adding bay leaves, birds' eyes, and virgin hair. He was more efficient this time instead of fueled by blinding rage and a newly broken heart. Dark birds flew out from the black smoke and seeped into his vial, ready to bend to his will when freed. Every so often, he cast a glance at Rozlyn, who took it upon herself to not make one doll but *five*.

"Marquis, the sun has risen," Iseult announced from the doorway. "And we have returned to the Dawnbreak Court."

Fuck!

Haven gripped the corked vial on the shelf and brushed past his assistant to the front entrance of the tower. He released his shadows, but the door didn't budge against their rough attempts to open it. Hot blood pulsing within his veins, he raced up the staircase to the top of the tower.

His magic stripped him of his shirt and boots as he entered the room. He went out to the window ledge, freed his gargoyle, then barreled forward with a hard snap of his wings. A gust of wind struck him like a wall, boomeranging him back into the room.

The binding hadn't altered this part at all.

Haven growled to himself as Rozlyn stepped through the doorway.

Jaw clenched, he released a shadow that curled toward her. "I need two tendrils of hair this time."

7

ROZLYN

Day in and day out, for two weeks, Rozlyn assisted the Marquis of Shadows as he attempted to come up with a spell to make his curse fade properly so he wasn't trapped in his home at all. But each morning when Haven tried to fly outside the tower window, the wind tossed him back into the room like a raggedy old garment. There had been another spell he'd come up with by using drops of their blood and locks of their hair that was meant to firmly root the tower within the Souldark Court, but it was another failure. Two tendrils of her hair inside Haven's locket hadn't improved the situation in the least.

Rozlyn couldn't pinpoint why these spells were failing when the marquis' sorcery didn't seem flawed in any other aspect, but she couldn't be completely certain. She was no sorceress.

Between the times when Haven asked for a lock of her hair, and another, and another, and *another*, Rozlyn took dresses from the wardrobe at the top of the tower and fashioned the dark gowns into something more welcoming, regardless of the marquis' favorite drab color. Sequins and glistening beads easily added a little jovialness to them. More lace fashioned along the sleeves, hems, and neckline gave them liveliness over death.

Rozlyn sat in a velvet chair, its cushions akin to clouds, within the spell room while Haven, wearing his beloved frown, hovered over the metal cauldron. He adorned a long-sleeved button-up shirt tucked into dark trousers that she couldn't deny hugged his backside rather well. His long white hair fell into his face once more, and he cursed it as he snatched a strip of leather from a nearby shelf to tie it back.

Fighting a smile, Rozlyn lifted the dress she'd been working on ever since night first fell. She slid the needle in and out of the lush fabric as she attached the lace around the linen hem. Before she looped the thread into a knot, a hand, a rather large masculine one, appeared in front of her face, and she glanced up to find a deep line settled between Haven's dark brows.

"Another lock of hair," he said, the coal-black shadow unraveling from his palm, inching nearer to her.

"Patience is not your virtue," Rozlyn huffed and

completed her task on the dress first. "There. Finished," she sang and folded the fabric in her lap, then drew her plait over her shoulder and held the ends up for his shadow. The deep red color was growing on her, although she missed the golden hue dearly.

Haven's shadow inched closer, brushing her hand in a soft caress as it drifted toward her hair. She shivered at the gentle touch, not knowing it would feel so heavenly soft. Scissor blades formed from the shadow before it snipped off a tendril. As Haven clutched her hair in his fist, the marquis' gaze fixed on her dress, his expression unreadable.

"Do you like it?" Rozlyn asked, trailing her fingers across a perfect line of black pearl buttons down the back.

With a grunt, he sauntered to the cauldron, and by his lack of commenting, she took the reply as a most certainly.

Haven tossed her hair into the contents, then opened a golden jar and poured in a metallic blue liquid. A pungent odor drifted through the air, and she covered her nose.

"Fuck," he spat, slapping a hand against his leg. Waving his arm through the air, the smell vanished, replaced by a pleasant leather.

Rozlyn laid the dress on the chair and slipped beside the marquis, watching the bloody liquid in the cauldron bubble and burst. "You know," she said slowly. "I think you need to find someone who can help you solve your predicament. You're becoming emotionally driven over your curse, and that obsession isn't going to improve the situation. Impulsive behavior might turn you into a stone gargoyle again, but *this time* it might last all night as well. I don't believe you would like that at all."

Haven's scowl deepened as he cocked his head, seeming to mull over her words. "There's no one to ask, maiden. I've never once had trouble with sorcery, other than the spell that got me into this fucking situation."

"Don't you have family somewhere? Friends?" With being as well-known as he was, there had to be *someone*.

"My parents are dead. Iseult's skeleton would break apart before he found anyone who could do half the things I can, and as for friends, I've only ever had Vivienne…" Haven trailed off. But he didn't have to finish the sentence for her to know Vivienne was his lover who chose to marry the Lord of Souldark.

Silence stretched between them, and Haven sank down at his work table, where he placed a bowl of green liquid on its surface. He then pushed a stack of books aside to grab a few jars off the shelf. Beaks, brown leaves, scales, and an orange powder.

Rozlyn wrinkled her nose as she watched Haven mix the ingredients into the liquid. "Is this for a different spell?" The other ones had all been ingredients added to the main cauldron's bloody liquid.

"Yes," he said, dropping the leaves into the bowl. "I'm taking a break for now."

She pursed her lips and blinked. If he was going to poke around for weeks on end and not solve this matter, he would get nowhere, which meant she would remain in this tower. When Rozlyn accepted the offer to come to the Marquis of Shadows' home, she never would've imagined that it was waiting for a curse he was under to completely fade. She'd assumed there would've been nights filled with pleasure, then after their dalliances were finished, she would've bid the sorcerer a happy farewell before smiling on her way to purchase a dress shop.

Rozlyn chose to focus on Haven's admission. Vivienne. She wouldn't dare bring up the lord or the lady at that moment, but Vivienne was his friend once. Rozlyn could travel to the castle and meet with the Lady of Souldark. For Haven's sake, she needed to do something other than watch the marquis growl at himself over failed spells. If she revealed her plan to him, she knew for a fact the sorcerer would make certain she couldn't leave his home. And *that* wouldn't do in the least.

She smoothed out the skirts of her dress, lifted her satchel of sewing supplies, and casually yawned. "I'm going to work on a few of the gowns upstairs after grabbing something to eat. Perhaps even a bath. Do you still need my assistance?"

Haven's pale eyes met hers, his gaze veering down to her mouth. And were his pupils dilating? "Not now," Haven mumbled and looked away before she could clarify if there had perhaps been lust lingering for a moment.

He was a very handsome grouch indeed.

As Rozlyn entered the kitchen, dishes clinked as Iseult placed them inside a glass cabinet.

"Hello, Rozlyn," he said, then resumed organizing the shelves.

"Hello!" she chirped.

The scent of delicious bread and desserts permeated the large space, and she took a frosted cherry pastry from a plate on the counter. She bit into its wonderful sweetness and wiped a few crumbs from her lips. As Iseult went to the next cabinet, she stuffed jerky and a few pieces of fruit into her satchel. She asked the room for a canteen of water, then placed that inside her bag too. With the landscape being so barren around the tower, she wasn't quite sure when she could fill it again.

Rozlyn smiled brightly as she stood beside Haven's skeletal assistant. "I was wondering if I may have your opinion on some of the dresses upstairs. There's a new design I'd like to try."

Iseult's skull turned in her direction, his jaw parted. "I'm not to wear them, am I?"

"No." She laughed softly. "Not unless you want to, that is. They might be a little short on you though."

Iseult pressed a bony hand to the front of his dark robes. "No, I like what Marquis gave me to wear. But yes, it will be my honor to assist you in whatever you need."

Her chest tightened that she was about to trick him,

yet she did owe him a favor for slipping a sleeping aid into her tea that first day.

Iseult followed Rozlyn up the winding staircase, the violet flames flickering in their sconces, making the shadows dance along the walls.

Once they stood before the towering wardrobe, she drew open the doors to the assortment of dark gowns. She took a silk sash from the waist of a lacy garment and folded her arms as though contemplating which dress to choose.

Rozlyn tsked, then pointed to a row of dresses in the far back of the wardrobe. "Pick one of those for me. I just can't decide!"

"They all look similar." Iseult angled his skull to the side. "But let me inspect them more closely." He brushed past her and skimmed his skeletal finger across a satin dress, then chiffon. She slowly tiptoed in behind him, edging closer, her movements quiet.

As he reached for a wool dress with a sweetheart neckline, Rozlyn leapt forward and grabbed both of his arms, pulling them behind his spine. With how light and flimsy his arms were, she prayed to the gods she wouldn't break them off, but if she did, she would apologize and take faith that Haven's sorcery would mend him as it had when he'd leapt from the tower window to collect her at the brothel.

"What are you doing?" Iseult gasped, wriggling his fragile frame. Rozlyn grappled with his thin arms and bound the fabric around his wrists.

"I'm sorry," she breathed, her chest heaving as she tied the sash into tight knots, "but let's just say I owed you for the sleep aid you gave me when I arrived."

"Marquis!" Iseult shouted. "Marquis!"

That was something Rozlyn had already thought about, which was why the room in the upper tower was perfect since Haven wouldn't hear him from so far down below.

Rozlyn spun Iseult by the shoulders and held him against the dresses along the wardrobe's wall. Even if Iseult would last long enough to find help, he wouldn't be able to defend himself if he encountered something vile—a child could easily throw him if they wanted to.

"Hush, and listen to me. Please," Rozlyn said, keeping her voice even. "I'm doing this for the marquis. He needs outside help." If she didn't seek someone's aid, she feared this tower would be her home forever. Haven needed her hair daily, but if she were gone for a little while and returned successfully, a handful of days of him turning into a stone gargoyle would be nothing compared to years of being free of a curse.

Iseult stilled. "Marquis is going to be angry."

"Not if he's no longer trapped here all day," Rozlyn pointed out. "I can't leap from the window like Haven or you, so I need to borrow your key."

Iseult didn't writhe in her grasp as she fished out the silver key from inside his pocket.

Rozlyn slowly backed away, keeping her eyes trained on the shadows swirling within his sockets. "Stay here," she said. Iseult didn't move, his shoulders sagging as she grasped both doors and added, "Don't worry, when I return, we can trust each other from here on out."

Iseult sighed. "I do like you very much, Rozlyn."

"I like you too." Her heart clenched as she shut the wardrobe, then placed the brush from her satchel through its handles. Just in case.

As she gazed out of the window at the Souldark Court, she was thankful it was still night. She needed to hurry and leave before day broke and she was trapped inside the tower again. After placing the dagger at her hip, she grasped her skirts and rushed down the stairs toward the front entrance.

Pulse racing, she reached the last step and slid the key into the lock until it clicked. And although the noise was soft, it was akin to a boom inside her ears. She slowly opened the door to a mild creak, but no footsteps thundered from below.

Rozlyn poked her head out into the night, searching side to side for anything nefarious. Not a soul lingered anywhere in the mist near the tower. She locked the door behind her and darted off toward the forest of dead trees, their branches frail, their trunks curved and rotting.

She didn't know much about the other courts, but from the map of Grimm that Madam had given her as a child, the Souldark castle was far south near the sea.

Peering up at the sky, she followed the cluster of stars that would lead her in the southern direction. A part of her wanted to turn around and cross over the border into Dawnbreak, to run back to the brothel, but she couldn't leave the Marquis of Shadows cursed.

The heavy scent of smoke surrounded Rozlyn as she zigzagged around twig-like trees while gripping her knife. Gray spirits dotted the landscape in the thickening mist, but none of them charged after her. She caught sight of a strange horned creature, its scarlet body hunched and skin sagging as it tightened its grip around a spirit, inhaling its energy. The stories that Madam had told her mentioned how spirits wouldn't die since they were already dead, only lose parts of their memories at first. What came after that, she wasn't certain of.

Heart thrumming, Rozlyn barreled past a marsh and glimpsed spirits in a curving line at a glistening lake where a silver gondola sat empty. Her eyes widened at the one miraculous thing she'd seen thus far. The gateway to the gods. *Fairward.* She didn't stop her journey though, only kept going until a manor with white turrets slipped into view. Glistening orange orbs, like glass, floated around the home, their movements delicate and graceful. She craned her neck, wondering what they were for.

As her side and legs cramped, she slowed as she approached the home. She leaned against the manor's side wall to catch her breath when a deep voice purred from behind her, "Why you're not a spirit, are you?"

Lips parting, Rozlyn whirled around and lifted her blade. "No, I'm not."

"A blade isn't necessary." The man stepped out from the shadows—he wasn't a spirit either. His silver hair hung loosely past his chin, and midnight black eyes held amusement. He was a different kind of handsome than Haven, more otherworldly, his bronze skin flawless beneath the moon's illumination.

Rozlyn didn't lower her dagger. "Are you a sorcerer? Only sorcerers can come to Souldark." Unless he was here in the way she was.

"Not a sorcerer exactly." He cocked his head and smiled, his frame taller than Haven. "Why are you here?"

"I need to reach the Lady of Souldark. Can you help me?" Even though this man was a stranger, he could know of a faster route to the castle.

"I can accompany you for a little while if you wish. For a cost, that is." His gaze grew hooded and traveled down her form, then halted on her left wrist. "Oh, you belong to Haven … for the time being."

Rozlyn blinked, squaring her shoulders. "How do you know Haven?"

He smirked. "I'm the ferryman, but you can call me Nightshade."

She gasped. The *ferryman*. Madam had told her tales of him as well when Rozlyn was younger, about how he was immortal. While the lords were mortal and died here, the ferryman lived on, never changing as centuries passed. He was the unwanted bastard child of a god and mortal, which was one of the reasons Rozlyn remembered the stories about him so much. Because she'd related to him without them ever meeting.

"I'm Rozlyn." She smiled, lowering her knife a fraction.

"You don't want to travel to the castle tonight," he said. "Come inside my home, and I'll explain."

Rozlyn furrowed her brow. However, she'd done well with the training Madam gave her for defense.

"I won't hurt you," he added.

Anyone could promise that, but she nodded and allowed Nightshade to lead her around the side of the manor to the front door, where crumbling stone rested in two piles.

"Ignore that. A guest threw a bit of a tantrum the other week." He chuckled and pushed open the entrance.

As she stepped over the threshold behind the ferryman, she entered a sitting room with a staircase leading to the next floor. Orange flames crackled within a large fireplace where a fur rug rested. A velvet settee lingered across from two chaises, and a bronze table at their center held two glasses of wine. Silver metal vines snaked across the walls, creating a luxurious and nature-like feel at the same time.

Nightshade sat on the settee and handed her one of the wine glasses while taking a long, inviting sip from the other.

Rozlyn set the glass back on the table—she knew when a man wanted to lure in a woman for pleasure. "I'm bound to Haven and will not be seduced."

"Hmm." The corners of his lips lifted as he reclined back against the cushions.

She placed her hands on her hips and stepped toward him. "Now tell me why I don't want to go to the castle. Haven's under a curse, and it's urgent I speak with the lady of this court as soon as possible."

"*Haven* is under a curse?" He chuckled softly. "It seems you're unaware that his curse is your curse."

HAVEN

The marriage cuff squeezed Haven's wrist again, and he continued to ignore the forsaken thing. Apparently, it wanted Rozlyn at his heels. Or him at hers. The dress she'd been wearing hugged her breasts and waist in a way that had made his cock stiffen.

Haven pricked his finger and squeezed two drops of blood into the mixture. He unbound his hair and plucked a single strand before adding it to the liquid. Leaning over the bowl, he exhaled and let the concoction steal some of his breath. He'd told Rozlyn he needed a break from the other spell, but what he'd truly needed was a distraction from watching her out of the corner of his eye while at the cauldron. Every time she leaned over to stitch into the fabric, her cleavage nearly spilled out of her gown, begging him to give into temptation. To touch. To taste. To fuck.

No.

He stood from the chair and carried the bowl to one of the smaller cauldrons filled with herb-infused water, the talons of a dragon, the horn of a unicorn, and the bones of a wolf—all shifters from various courts.

Stirring the liquid in the cauldron first, he then poured the bowl's contents into the mixture. His shadows churned the liquid, around and around. Emerald smoke curled up from the cauldron, and he grabbed a vial from the shelf behind him. The smoke grew thicker and wove around the cauldron, remaining there and awaiting his call.

Haven held up the vial. "Enter," he demanded. The smoke listened and seeped into the glass until it was filled. A necromancy spell that he could easily sell to someone who was foolish enough to use it.

Once he was free of this curse.

But waking the dead never turned out well for those gullible enough to follow through with it.

He looked at the successful spell on his shelf that was still waiting to be used on Adham. *Soon.*

Haven's gaze fell on the chair where Rozlyn had been seated, the dress she'd been working on neatly strewn across. He was used to seeing her in here, listening to the soft sounds of the pads of her fingertips brushing fabrics and sliding a needle in and out of it. The room suddenly felt empty now. But why would he give a fuck? Did he want to preen to her over the spell he'd just completed? *Pathetic.* He'd always lingered alone in here before, even when he'd been with Vivienne. Now that he thought about it, over the past couple of weeks, he'd spent more time in this room with Rozlyn than he ever had with his match.

Haven flexed and unflexed his hands, then went to the cauldron in the corner to distract himself. White and black bubbles speckled the blood. Furrowing his brow, he dipped the ladle into the thick liquid and scooped up Rozlyn's hair. He lifted the lock between his fingers and rubbed the crimson away until deep purple strands were revealed. Another failure. In every instance her locks had turned a color other than the red he'd wanted to remain.

"Fuck," he grunted, then threw the hair back into the cauldron and wiped the blood from his hand with a towel. There had to be something he could do to keep the tendrils inside his locket from turning back to gold. If the hair within the cauldron remained the shade of blood, he could use it to stay out of the tower for more than a day. Eventually he wouldn't need Rozlyn or her hair at all. *But fucking when?*

Haven should've only had to marry the bastard princess and use her hair once, not continue searching for an answer to solve this endless riddle. He swiped his hand across glass jars on the shelf, letting them shatter against the floor, the sound utterly satisfying. Jaw tight, he snapped his fingers and the glass and contents slid together, the jars perfectly back on the shelf.

His eyes rolled to the ceiling, and he pinched the bridge of his nose—he needed another lock of Rozlyn's hair. But did he? Or was he attempting to make excuses to see her? The cuff squeezed his wrist as though agreeing for him to start over on the spell.

As he left the room, Haven wondered if Rozlyn had already taken a bath. Had she touched herself while in the evergreen-scented water, sliding delicate fingers between her folds, then slipping one, or two, into her wet pussy? When she found pleasure, how loud did she become? Soft and breathy or screaming and moaning? Did the water slosh against her large breasts, her hard nipples? And then he recalled how she didn't pleasure herself, only when she'd been learning. She saved her pussy to be touched by others, had come to his tower for *him* to touch *her*. His cock started to harden as it had earlier and he squeezed his balls until they ached. "Control yourself."

Rozlyn mentioned how Haven had been overly emotional while in the spell room, but he was pent-up with an extreme desire to fuck and fuck hard. Feel a warm cunt clench around his cock. He'd have to use his hand twice a day instead of once until reuniting with Vivienne.

Haven reached the top of the tower and pounded on the door. "Maiden."

"Marquis! Marquis!" Iseult shouted, his voice

muffled.

Was his assistant *touching* what was his? Was she attracted to a fucking *skeleton* this whole time? Haven threw open the door and discovered the room empty, but then the wardrobe rattled and he noticed a hairbrush stuck through the handles. He ripped the brush away, then yanked open the doors. Iseult tumbled to the floor, his wrists bound with a sash.

"Rozlyn left, Marquis. I couldn't stop her," he panted.

Haven's nostrils flared and he stared hard at his cuff, ignoring Iseult's rant about how Rozlyn was only trying to help. He hadn't once thought of checking the link between them, particularly since every time she was at the top of the tower and he below, it squeezed. Like a second pulse in his veins, the link thrummed, and he focused on it, feeling her. She was still in Souldark. But somewhere he hadn't expected. At least not yet. *Nightshade's* manor.

Was Rozlyn fucking *him*? How did she even get there? Had that slithering snake been visiting her in the tower somehow, buttering her up? She didn't belong to that bastard yet—she was still *his*. His princess, his captive, his *wife*.

"How did she get out?" Haven said between gritted teeth and balled his hands into tight fists.

"My key." Iseult sighed, his fingers clicking together behind his back. His assistant might've been tall, but Rozlyn could've overpowered him—anyone with hands could. Yet the fool shouldn't have been such an imbecile as to get himself trapped in the first place.

"Find a way to unbind yourself—I'm going to retrieve *my wife*," Haven growled.

Going after her in gargoyle form wouldn't be quick enough, especially not if she left Nightshade's manor and ventured further south. Who knew if this naïve maiden would get herself killed in Souldark. If she did, Haven would be fucked.

Besides locating her, the cuff was good for one other thing. He shut his eyes, muttering an incantation as his thumb ring drew out his shadows, the cuff digging into his flesh.

This spell better work.

A gust of wind swirled around him, tugging at each of his nerves, and when he opened his eyes, he was no longer in the tower room but in Nightshade's piece of shit manor. The fire crackled behind him, and his gaze settled on the ferryman. Nightshade smirked at him as he set his glass of wine on the table. Rozlyn stood near the settee, blinking at Haven, her pouty lips parted in surprise. They were both fully clothed, but his home still reeked of sex.

"What did you do to her?" Haven seethed as he stormed toward Nightshade, lifted him by the collar, and slammed him against the wall.

"Haven! Let him go," Rozlyn shouted. "You're acting ridiculous."

Nightshade grinned. "Yes, let me go." He leaned in close so only Haven could hear him. "We haven't fucked.

Yet."

Haven strained to keep his shadows from tearing Nightshade into tiny morsels. He released him and whirled on Rozlyn, his eyes narrowed. "You left the tower. Do you have a death wish?"

She squared her shoulders. "Are you threatening me?"

"Have I hurt you yet?" He frowned. "This court is dangerous. You need to stay in the tower—if you die, I'm fucked."

Rozlyn stepped toward him wearing a scowl that didn't suit her soft features. "Nightshade told me that your curse is now my curse. Is that true?"

That meddlesome prick. Haven's nostrils flared as he cast a murderous stare at Nightshade. "You—"

With an arched brow, the ferryman tapped the tattoo on his wrist, prompting Haven to recall that they had a bargain—meaning he would tell Rozlyn all of it. And that could interfere with Haven's plan.

"Wait in the corner over there," Haven said to Rozlyn, motioning to a spot on the opposite side of the room, then faced Nightshade.

The ferryman's smile widened as he looked past him, but before Haven could turn around, Rozlyn's smaller, albeit strong, form leapt onto his back. He stumbled forward, tripping over Nightshade's fur rug, until they collapsed into a heap on the floor. Even though he was larger than her, she flipped him onto his back and pinned him down by the shoulders, a dagger at his throat.

"My madam taught me how to be nice, but she also taught me how to be very bad when needed." She tilted her head and smiled innocently. "So now, Marquis, we'll discuss this curse situation thoroughly, or I'll make your night far worse than you've ever imagined."

A low chuckle rumbled up Haven's throat. This bastard princess may be a better physical fighter than him, but she was no match for his sorcery. He could easily have his shadows remove her from him and hold her against the wall. But he didn't. A lick of heat veered straight to his cock, and regardless of what his future plans were, he wanted to fuck her right there.

"Don't mind me," Nightshade purred, reminding Haven whose home he was in. The fucker picked up his wine glass from the table and sipped on it while peering down at Haven and Rozlyn.

Haven's gaze met Rozlyn's brown eyes, and in this light, they appeared nearly hazel. "We'll have a discussion," he started, "but I need to speak with Nightshade first."

"Fine," she relented, "but if you don't tell me the truth about the curse, I'll slice one of your fingers off, then stitch it back on."

Haven fought a smile. "You need to practice your threats, maiden."

Rozlyn huffed and removed the blade from his throat. She then peeled her curvy body off his, leaving him desiring her warmth as she went to the corner of the room.

He pushed himself up from the floor and approached Nightshade. "You asshole," Haven ground out.

"Follow me," Nightshade said and lured him into the shadows of a dim hallway. He leaned against the wall and grinned. "You didn't say how tempting the princess was. I quite like our bargain."

"Shut your mouth," Haven snapped.

"If I didn't know any better, I'd say you *fancy* her." He chuckled. "But how could that be when you claim Vivienne is your perfect match?"

A deep growl escaped Haven's throat. "Silence."

Unfazed, Nightshade brought the glass to his lips and finished his wine. "At our last meeting, I forgot to mention that there's someone who might be able to help with your curse."

Haven glowered. "What are you talking about?"

"A spirit resides at the bog near the white mountain," the ferryman drawled. "An ancient sorcerer."

"And you just *happened* to forget about him?"

"It slipped my mind. I was focused on other things that night. Fucking. Wine. *Bargains*." He shrugged. "Figured you would come back. You never did."

"You're playing games," Haven said, his voice low, dangerous.

"Aren't we all?" He peered past him into the sitting room. "I think you have a *wife* to return to."

"If you're fucking with me about this sorcerer, my

shadows will eat you alive," Haven vowed.

"You and your shadows will thank me." He leaned in close and cooed, "And I'll thank you when Rozlyn is mine. You might want to fuck her while you have the chance."

Gritting his teeth, Haven turned and left Nightshade lurking in the shadows. Rozlyn was still in the corner, chewing on her plump lip while stitching a yellow piece of cloth.

"This isn't the time to be sewing," Haven muttered.

"It's the perfect time," she said without looking up. "I left the tower to help *you*."

Sunlight spilled through the slit between the curtains, and Haven held up a finger. "We'll continue this conversation when we're back in the tower."

Bright light flashed before his eyes, and as it cleared, he and Rozlyn were no longer at Nightshade's manor but inside the room at the top of his tower.

9

ROZLYN

"We're back in the tower!" Rozlyn gasped, the small square of fabric falling from her fingertips and drifting to the floor. She stared around the familiar dark-as-night room, the wardrobe now open. But only she and Haven stood there. No sign of Iseult or Nightshade.

"So we are." Haven scowled, his pale eyes slitted. "You disobeyed me, maiden."

She blinked. "You never said I couldn't leave temporarily!"

"I wasn't aware I had to be so specific," he ground out.

"I would've asked, but you would've said no!" Her voice rose, coming out high-pitched at the tail end.

"Of course I would've. You need to stay *here* where nothing can happen to you." He stepped closer, his head dipping toward hers so his nose was dangerously close to brushing hers. His citrusy scent enveloped her, the perfect blend of both sour and sweet, and although he had never been the second of the two, the smell matched him well.

"Instead, I find you in the ferryman's manor when you're *my* wife," he continued.

Rozlyn jabbed a finger against his chest. "I wasn't there to pleasure him. I was there to find a way to help your too-proud self since you were unwilling to do so. You should be grateful that someone wanted to help you."

Haven caught her wrist, his fingers digging into her marriage cuff. "Don't do it again."

"I do believe this curse has turned you into a spoiled child. Unless this is how you've always been," she said, wiggling out of his hold.

He remained quiet, his nostrils flaring as he inwardly brooded. The sunlight spilling through the window drew her attention, and Rozlyn pursed her lips as she opened the glass to peer out. To no surprise, the tower was once again in the Dawnbreak Court, the lush foliage sweeping across the land, the dark birds drawn to the tower like a moth to a flame.

As Nightshade stated—Haven's curse was her curse.

Rozlyn dug her fingernails into her palms until they

were the deepest crescent moons she could make. She'd known that the tower wouldn't allow the entrance door to open during the day because of the ruckus the Marquis of Shadows had created by jumbling a spell, but she'd believed she wasn't truly trapped here in the way he was. And at some point, regardless of the marriage cuff, if she'd had enough of this life, wanted to give up any future payment, she could've bid him a final goodbye, gone out the door at nightfall, and crossed over the border into Dawnbreak. Not be transported back to the tower as Haven had been!

Even though he'd been demanding, had tricked her into being his wife, she'd wanted to help him, to make his scowl vanish. If she'd cursed herself to a tower for two years, her demeanor might've changed in the same way his had. She'd always heard that the Marquis of Shadows was a man of few words, got what he wanted, and if one crossed him, well, they wouldn't live to tell the tale.

Haven remained quiet behind her, but she could feel him glaring daggers at her back. Yet she should be the one glaring! She'd left the tower, risked her life, to *help* him, even if it was for nothing in the end. Or no, she'd uncovered the truth, so she was no longer so naïve.

After resting her satchel on the floor, she took a deep breath and placed her hands against the window sill, then lifted herself out toward the ledge. Before her foot could brush the stone, Haven's strong arms wrapped around her waist, pulling her back inside. Only, he didn't set her on the floor—he cradled her in his arms against his chest with a firm grip, his blazing pale eyes trained on hers as if she might disappear from him once more.

"Why are you such a careless woman?" He bared his teeth, his face shifting into gargoyle form for a brief moment. "You will not keep me trapped here by getting yourself killed."

Laughter bubbled up Rozlyn's throat, and she patted his cheek, his stubble tickling her palm. "Is that what you believed I was doing?"

"Why else would you be out there? You have no wings," he said gruffly.

"Even if I decided to leap from the tower and end my life, that is my choice. Not yours, Haven," Rozlyn stated, her tone serious. "But no, I only wanted to see if I would be pushed back inside by the wind too." She placed a hand against his pompous mouth before he could speak. "If I slipped, you would've turned into your gargoyle and caught me before I struck the earth."

She removed her hand so he could now speak. "Another foolish thought." His warm breath mingled with Rozlyn's, and his heavy gaze remained on hers until he was the first to break away.

"Since we have that settled, I will continue and see for myself." Rozlyn wiggled from his arms, and he glowered but let her slide down from him so she could climb out the window.

As she stood on the ledge, a flock of ravens circled

the tower, their shrill sounds reverberating throughout the forest. The wind tousled the ends of her long plait— her stomach plummeted, her heart lodged in her throat, and she trembled as she peered down at the grass below. Heights had never been her forte.

"You're shaking like a leaf," Haven muttered.

"You have a wild imagination," she stammered, clutching the stone of the window for dear life.

Haven grasped her wrist but didn't yank her inside, only kept her from making a mishap. Still, it steadied her, and she slowly breathed in and out.

"We don't have all day," he said.

"Oh, but we do have all day," she refuted. "We're both cursed here, or did you forget?"

Unintelligible words escaped him, and she smiled. She lifted her foot and leaned forward to take a step against emptiness, when a burst of wind slammed into her like stone, plastering her against the tower wall.

And *that* was the only proof she needed. Rozlyn was indeed trapped in the Marquis of Shadows' home like him. Or at least a prisoner during daylight.

"Get inside, maiden." Haven didn't wait for her response and gently tugged her through the window. "Enough foolishness."

"I had to make certain," she said, brushing the dirt from her dress. "You've left important truths out. More than once, I might add."

Haven admitted nothing and held out his hand, his

shadow unraveling from the depths beneath the marquis' flesh. It wafted in his palm, hovering like smoke. "Hair," he demanded.

"You could ask nicely," she huffed. "I could deny you after all."

He arched a brow and smirked. "Would you like us both to be stone gargoyles outside the tower? Do you prefer the left or right side of the window? Your choice."

Rozlyn held her tongue since words would do no good in this circumstance. She retrieved the scissors from her satchel, snipped a lock of red hair, and threw it at his feet.

"Well, that wasn't *nice* of you." The edges of Haven's lips curled up, and she reprimanded herself for thinking how much more handsome he appeared in that moment as he picked up her hair. He replaced the golden curl in his locket, his heavy stare returning to hers. "Since you trapped my assistant in your wardrobe and ran off without my knowledge, it's clear I can't trust you." He snapped his fingers and two shadows slithered out of his chest, one seeping through the floor and the other crawling up the window to encase the open space in inky darkness. "You won't sneak out again."

Rozlyn pressed her hand against the shadow cloaking the window. The shadow didn't budge at all—as if it were made from stone. "You're holding me prisoner now?" she hissed, whirling around on him.

"Did you assume I wasn't before? I didn't think to

spell that out for you, but it seems you don't take subtleties well." He shrugged.

"Were you this controlling with Vivienne?" Rozlyn asked, unable to keep the lady's name from slipping.

"Controlling?" Haven scoffed. "What have I done that's so terrible? The hair I take grows back. You've been able to fiddle around with garments all night instead of fucking strangers at the brothel. In the end, you'll be paid a fortune for your time here. And what do I ask from you? Simply to stay put. At the end of the day, you should be *thanking* me."

What an arrogant man! "I'm still cursed!" she shouted, waving her hands in his face. "Which was done without my knowledge, I might add."

"Most curses aren't preceded by a warning." Haven rolled his eyes. "Besides, it will be lifted eventually, we will be unwed, and then you'll be free of me and this tower."

Rozlyn bit the inside of her cheek. She *had* freely come to the tower, knowing that sorcerers held power, that the marquis hadn't come outside his home in two years. It was her fault for not asking enough questions and taking a leap of faith to achieve her dream. And although she may have been naïve, he'd still *tricked* her.

"Tonight," he continued, "when I leave, you will be obedient with Iseult."

Rozlyn thought about how she'd easily pinned the marquis down at Nightshade's... She perked up, folding her hands in front of her. "I can come with you. Your fighting skills aren't up to par, and I could watch your back in Souldark."

Haven shook his head. "Your place is in this tower."

"I'm only offering my help, is all." She sighed.

"I don't want your fucking help," he said. "What you did last night by going to the ferryman's was the opposite of helpful."

"I didn't leave here to see *him*," she drew out slowly. "I was on my way to the castle to find Vivienne."

"*Vivienne*," he seethed, his hands gripping his hair as he angrily paced across the room before stomping back toward her. "You would've ruined *everything*."

The way his nostrils flared, his eyes blazed like a crackling fire, and his face stained scarlet might've made anyone else cower. But he was all bark and no bite with her, and besides that, he already admitted he needed her.

"You two were close before, and she's a sorceress," Rozlyn murmured. "I figured she might hold more power since she's married to the Lord of Souldark."

"Fuck Adham," he snarled. "That bastard will pay soon enough."

Rozlyn blinked, understanding crashing into her like a massive sea wave. She mulled over every interaction she'd had with the marquis since coming to this tower— Haven's desperation to remain in Souldark, his annoyance at dawn every day, and not only because he was trapped in his home, but because they weren't in the barren court. It shouldn't have mattered where the tower was located as long as the spell could be broken. Yet Vivienne was in Souldark, and the Marquis of Shadows didn't care that she was married to the lord. He didn't want to move on and get over his old lover.

"You want Vivienne back," she whispered. "You want to remove the lord from her life and have her choose you."

Haven's jaw tightened, and he didn't deny it or spin an untruth.

"You can't force people to return your affections," Rozlyn said softly and placed her hand against his arm. He didn't jerk out of her touch, only remained quiet as she thought of her patron Lucius and how she'd only ever cared for him as a friend. Nothing more. Lucius couldn't make her love him, just as Haven couldn't make Vivienne. "Murdering the lord will only make Vivienne hate you. Patrons wish for courtesans to love them all the time, but they rarely ever do." They were taught not to, and that was to protect both the hearts of the courtesans and their patrons.

"Don't ever mention anything of love again. You know what your duty is to me." His voice came out low, deadly, as he backed away from her, then slammed the door behind him, leaving her alone.

Rozlyn's shoulders fell. "A broken man with a broken heart." Even though she'd never met Vivienne, killing the lord would be a cruel fate for her. Haven needed time to himself, and Rozlyn needed sleep after a long night.

Draping her long plait over her shoulder, Rozlyn unbound her hair, then removed her boots. As she padded toward the bed, a gentle knock came at the door. Was Haven coming to apologize to her? It would be very unlike him to do so. And her assumptions were accurate when she opened the door to find Iseult standing before her with a tray of biscuits, berries, and tea in his skeletal hand.

"You promised when you returned that we would trust each other," he said. "I believe we may start now."

She nodded with a small smile. "We may. I'm sorry again for earlier. I hope Haven wasn't angry with you."

"Fear not, my duties remain the same to Marquis. I'm happy." It was clear in his tone that he sincerely cared about Haven—someone needed to.

"Did you know that I'm cursed too?" she asked. His answer wouldn't make a difference since they were starting fresh, but she still would like to know.

Iseult's jaw parted in surprise and he shook his head. "I'm Marquis' assistant. That is all. He doesn't confide in all things with me, but he is my priority. And now, so are you, Rozlyn."

Her chest tightened at how innocent and loyal he was. "Thank you." Her smile spread her cheeks. If her family at the brothel ever got to truly know Iseult, they would absolutely adore him.

He placed the food tray in her hands. "Get some rest. I must prepare the spell room for when you and Marquis awake."

Rozlyn bid him farewell and set the tray on the night table. She ate a warm buttered biscuit and drank down the chamomile tea before peeling the dress from her body and slipping beneath the silken sheets.

As Rozlyn closed her eyes, she smiled while imagining herself in her very own shop with wall-to-wall beautiful dresses. She counted gown after gown to drift off into sleep, but her thoughts continued to turn toward the Marquis of Shadows, wondering what he was like when he'd been Vivienne's lover.

HAVEN

Haven carried a crate of herbs for Vivienne as he walked her home from training. The sun shone down, highlighting Vivienne's heart-shaped face and her silky dark hair hanging past her shoulders. Her sorcery skills were improving, and she'd impressed him today. Being matched to her was going rather well, albeit slowly. It had been seven years and they'd only officially began courting a year ago. He was ready to move forward with her...

"I want us to live together in my tower," Haven said.

Vivienne halted and grasped his arm, her emerald eyes meeting his. "It's too soon. I don't want to ruin our friendship."

"There's nothing you can do wrong. Our sorcery will work wonders together," he vowed.

Haven jolted forward in bed, gripping his damp hair

so hard his scalp throbbed. "Fuck. I was wrong," he rasped into the pitch-black room.

The marriage cuff squeezed Haven's wrist, alerting him that there was a different woman in his tower, one who wasn't Vivienne—his match—the one who *should've* been his wife. He swore to himself he would reclaim her, but he was reminded of the ridiculous night before. He blamed his high-strung emotions for the rage he felt thinking Rozlyn was fucking Nightshade. Even now, the thought of her pleasuring the ferryman made his blood boil, and his hands balled into tight fists. Why was he thinking of her like this? The need for a woman to sate his cock must've been driving him mad.

While she was his, Rozlyn would fuck no one—not until his curse was broken. Once he reunited with Vivienne, he wouldn't give a damn about the courtesan, and the mere memory of her face and body would disappear.

A soft knock came at the door and Haven snapped his fingers—a row of green flames ignited, licking the wicks of his black candles. He grabbed his shirt from the floor and fastened the buttons before he answered the door. Even though he generally dressed with sorcery, sometimes he just needed to move his fingers when his mind was overthinking.

Iseult wore his robes—the rope tied at his middle, which made him appear as though he had a waist. "The sun is down, Marquis."

"Good. And the maiden?"

"She's still asleep. Would you like me to wake her?" he asked.

Haven didn't need Rozlyn to distract his focus from Vivienne. "No, let her sleep," he said, brushing past his assistant and stepping out into the hallway. He turned back, his gaze meeting Iseult's shadowed sockets, and the marquis narrowed his eyes. "Do *not* get locked up again while I'm gone."

"Of course not, Marquis." He placed his skeletal palms together and bowed his head.

Haven rolled his eyes and left his assistant to himself. As he entered the kitchen, a silver flask and a hearty breakfast of eggs, bacon, sausage, and biscuits awaited him, even though Iseult knew he could've easily made something appear. He sat down on an iron stool and polished off his plate while staring at an unfinished silky garment Rozlyn had left behind on the counter. Did she sew in every room at the brothel too? Why was he even fucking wondering about that?

Once he drank half the whisky, it refilled and he tucked the flask into his trouser pocket for the long flight to the bog. Nightshade better have spoken the truth about the ancient sorcerer. The ferryman was the only one in Souldark who knew every spirit that lingered. Not even Adham knew without consulting Nightshade. Haven loathed to admit it, but Nightshade was more of a lord here than Adham had ever been.

But if the ferryman had tricked Haven to get him away from the tower so he could visit Rozlyn, he would find a way to brutally end the immortal. Haven trusted his spells and shadows would hold strong and prevent anyone from entering, but that wouldn't negate Nightshade's betrayal.

Fishing out a leather tie inside his other pocket, he drew his hair back and ascended the steps to the front entrance. As his shadow unlocked the door, Haven peered up the winding staircase leading to Rozlyn. He studied his cuff, feeling her still safely within the tower walls.

Haven knew he should just fucking leave, but he felt a need to see her first. He told himself it was only to confirm that she was indeed there. But, while bounding up the stairs, he couldn't help thinking about how her warm body had felt in his arms when he'd held her, how the swell of her right breast had pressed against his chest. Through her foolish behavior on the ledge of the tower, she'd made him almost smile, something only Vivienne had ever done.

Haven slowly opened the door, his sorcery keeping the hinges silent. The eternal flames flickered in their onyx sconces, illuminating Rozlyn's soft features in the corner of the room. He crept closer and swallowed deeply when he discovered her dress lay in a pool of fabric beside the bed. The silk blankets were drawn to her waist, exposing her pale skin and bare breasts. He stilled, his gaze lingering on her supple rosebud nipples a beat too long, pondering if they'd taste like sunshine too, before he cast his gaze up to her round face. If he hadn't been trapped in stone for two years and had decided to visit a brothel to get back at Vivienne, he would've chosen Rozlyn for a night of pleasure. Weeks ago, he had thought of her as nothing, but now, as he looked at her, he might be tempted enough to fuck her if she offered herself again.

His cock twitched as he studied her long lashes, her plump lips, still an alluring glossy black. Rozlyn shivered, and gooseflesh covered her arms. Haven should've walked away then, but his shadows warred with him, until finally, he allowed two translucent hands to slide out of him and draw the blankets up to her chin. He didn't want her to catch an illness and die before his curse lifted was all. Without her bound to him, collecting another bastard princess wouldn't be easy. And another might not be as civil as this one.

She sighed, content, no longer shivering. Even in sleep she looked like she was smiling, happy.

Whirling away from her as though he hadn't covered her at all, Haven opened the window while doing away with his shirt. When his hands brushed the window sill, a small, tired yawn pierced the air. "Haven?" Rozlyn called.

Haven shut his eyes tightly, warning himself not to glance back at her, not to fall into her trap if the blankets had fallen into her lap. Not ask if she wanted him to flick his tongue over her pebbled nipple.

"Don't do anything foolish while I'm gone," he said while slipping through the open space. Standing out on the ledge, he released his wings as his skin turned to a stark alabaster. Fully shifted into his gargoyle form, he leapt toward the sky and into the night.

Darkness surrounded him, the overcast sky cloaking the stars. He cracked his wings, flying away from the tower and over the mist rolling across the ground. Every so often the cuff squeezed his wrist like a noose, begging him to go back to Rozlyn.

Growls echoed from below as scaled monsters and horned beasts roamed the court. Spirits moaned, unable to find their way to Fairward Lake. Haven soared past the ferryman's gondola, the line shorter this time. But more spirits would come—death wouldn't stop unless the gods chose to end Grimm.

Haven flew over Nightshade's manor, and he watched as the ferryman led a spirit into his home. Once Rozlyn became Nightshade's, would the ferryman continue to fuck any spirit who lusted after him? Of course he would.

After hours of traveling through the wretched court, Haven sipped from his flask. He needed to reach the bog before sunrise, and if he didn't get there in time, the only other option was to demand Nightshade bring the ancient sorcerer to the tower.

Two dried-up streams came into view when the heavy stench of spoiled milk invaded Haven's nostrils. *The bog.* Just up ahead.

Tufts of gray decayed plant matter poked up from the murky water. A single, large hut rested between the bog and thin trees.

Haven descended, his clawed feet shifting and boots appearing before he planted into the muddy ground. The stench grew bolder, and his gaze locked onto the hut. Twigs weaved and molded together made up the outer walls of the home, and a thatched roof rested atop. He arched a brow at the pitiful home, wondering if Nightshade had lied about an ancient sorcerer residing here.

Tucking the remainder of his gargoyle form away, he prowled toward the hut, his shadows swirling inside him, ready to do his bidding.

Haven pounded on the door, and a moment later a gray spirit walked through the wall. The man's hair hung in disarray just past his shoulders, and bushy eyebrows hovered over his beady eyes.

"Who are you?" the spirit asked. He was a head shorter than Haven, but the marquis could feel the sorcery radiating from the beaded bracelet around the man's wrist.

"They call me the Marquis of Shadows," Haven drawled, releasing his dark silhouettes. They curled from his chest and swirled around him like hissing vipers. "The ferryman sent me here. I was told you are an ancient sorcerer and might be able to help me."

"The ferryman, hmm?" The spirit scratched his chin.

"Did he tell you who I am?"

"Does it matter?" Haven asked.

The spirit puffed his chest up proudly. "I'm Duke Phoenix Yashine, and I once hailed from the Sunwraith Court."

Haven had heard of him, of his strength, but the sorcerer had died centuries before he was born. He'd burned himself at a stake, refusing to be a pawn to any court.

Perhaps Nightshade had led him in the right direction after all. "So you *can* help me then," Haven said.

The man clucked his tongue. "If I can, what will you give me in return?"

Another fucking bargain. One had been plenty, but there was only one thing all spirits wanted badly enough to bargain. Especially one who had resided here this long with his memories intact. "A gondola ride across Fairward Lake to cross over to the gods."

"That isn't up to you," Phoenix said, but he sounded intrigued by the idea.

"If you help me, the ferryman will allow it. I'll make certain of it."

Phoenix studied Haven for a long moment, then motioned him forward. "Come in. It's too dangerous outside." The spirit passed through the wall as Haven's shadows drew open the door.

Clutter filled Phoenix's home—books strewn about and various-sized glass jars and vials piled into a corner.

A bed and a chair made from twigs were pushed up against a single wall. On a table in the center of the room rested a collection of more jars containing a variety of colored powders.

"Now," Phoenix said, plopping on the dirt in front of the table. "What do you need help with?"

"I rushed a spell and cursed myself," Haven muttered. "At first, I was a stone gargoyle during the day and trapped in my tower all night. I bound myself to a bastard princess using an old ceremony along with my own spell to reverse it, knowing the curse wouldn't dissipate completely at first. A lock of the princess's hair keeps it at bay. I'm free to leave my tower at night now, but during the day we're both imprisoned in it. The tower itself continues to return to her court instead of staying in Souldark."

Phoenix's brow furrowed. "You bound yourself to her, but did you consummate inside the tower or outside it? If the tower is where you're trapped, consummation would need to happen outside it. You would still require her hair daily until the curse completely fades, of course."

"We haven't consummated." Haven frowned, his pulse rushing through his veins when he recalled Rozlyn offering herself after he'd bound them together.

The spirit's smile grew, revealing several crooked teeth. "Ah, I believe you now have your answer then."

Haven's lips tightened into a thin line. The marriage was only meant to be temporary, and the binding spell was all that was required to make them husband and wife. But perhaps not if the curse was too strong... It only made sense that the most powerful sorcerer made a most powerful fucking curse.

"Go to the ferryman in the morning and tell him the Marquis of Shadows demands he take you to the gods," Haven said. Nightshade had tried to seduce Rozlyn when she didn't belong to him yet, so he owed him.

"Let's hope he does," Phoenix said. "I'll find you if he refuses."

Without another word, Haven left the ancient sorcerer's home. He dragged in a deep breath as he released his wings and surveyed the dreary woods before him. Was fucking Rozlyn a betrayal to Vivienne or a way to make them even? She'd fucked another man, and now he would fuck another woman, then his match would grovel at his feet. Vivienne was the only woman he'd pleasured, but he was left with no choice if it meant ending his curse. He thought about Rozlyn's plump lips, how her breasts would feel in his palms, how tight her pussy would feel around his cock.

He was a bastard and didn't give a damn.

The fucking would be simple, but the hair... It took longer than a day to travel to Adham's castle. If Phoenix was right and the curse would start to fade, maybe there was a simple solution. If Rozlyn traveled with him, he could get a new piece of her hair whenever the power of the first ran its course.

It was still dark, but if he hurried, he could fuck Rozlyn tonight. If she wanted more coin, he would promise it. After traveling with him to Adham's, she might not get to spend it, yet that wasn't his problem.

As he lifted his arm, a loud splash echoed behind him and he spun around, releasing his shadows just as a storm of small beads of light spread everywhere. *Will-o'-the-wisps.*

He focused on his cuff, on Rozlyn, and one moment he was near the bog—the next he was in the room at the top of the tower. But not before an explosion of sharp pain slashed through his wings.

"Fuck!" Haven growled, collapsing to the floor and meeting Rozlyn's wide-eyed stare.

She rushed to his side and gasped as her soft fingers brushed his arm. "Your wings are torn!"

11

ROZLYN

"Fuck!" Haven sneered for the second time and pushed up from the floor. "I'm going to murder them all."

Rozlyn snatched a dress from the floor and pressed the fabric against his wings to absorb the blood. She'd thought Haven had been upset about the curse again when he'd appeared in the room, but when her eyes had landed on his injuries, the thin membranes hanging like ripped curtains behind him, her heart clenched. As she lifted the fabric from his wounds, there wasn't as much blood as she'd expected.

"My gargoyle's skin is more resilient than my own and doesn't bleed for long," he rasped.

"What happened?" Rozlyn asked softly as she continued to dab two trickles of scarlet.

"I went to the bog," he ground out, pacing forward, and she had to catch up to him to wipe the lingering crimson. "And those fuckers came out of nowhere."

"I don't know who *those fuckers* are," Rozlyn said, balling up the bloody dress and placing it beside the door for the time being. "Spirits? Monsters?"

"Will-o'-the-wisps," Haven growled. "After I take care of Adham, I'll return to the bog to drown them all."

"Will-o'-the-wisps?" Rozlyn exclaimed. "I didn't even know they *existed*." In the eleven other courts, there were only shifters, the magical objects, and spells created by the sorcerers and sorceresses. The people of Grimm passed down fae bedtime stories to their children. Madam had told them to Rozlyn when she was younger as she fell asleep, but those were magical tales full of exciting adventures. The will-o'-the-wisps in them were kind, not vicious little beasts.

"They only live in Souldark. Apparently, they're remnants of the foliage when it was dying—the last bit of their life. And that life should be snuffed out." Haven squared his shoulders, his pale eyes blazing, not with pain or rage any longer, but something different... "Follow me outside. We need to fuck."

Rozlyn blinked, her lips parting in surprise. In the past few weeks, he hadn't once mentioned anything close to wanting to tumble, although she had wondered how his cock would feel inside her. On more than one occasion. "I'm sorry. *What?* I will oblige, but your wings are shredded, and you're thinking about pleasure at this very moment? You must be running a fever." She placed her palm against his forehead, and his skin was warm to the touch but no burning fever as she'd expected.

Haven clasped her wrist, his expression nearing desperate when he drew her toward the door. "I'm well enough. An ancient sorcerer gave me advice, and the only way I can leave the tower during the day is for us to consummate the marriage."

Rozlyn understood his desperation perfectly now. "Oh! That makes sense. So if we had bedded the night I offered myself to you, neither of us would've been trapped here?" Or she still would've been if she'd snuck off. But if he hadn't been cursed during the day, she might never have uncovered that his misery could be hers.

"Yes." Haven frowned. "I'll pay you double the coin. But—" He stilled as he looked toward the window, at the sunlight pouring into the room. He slapped his thigh and slowly ran a hand down his face. "Why can't anything fucking go as planned?"

Rozlyn patted his arm, his gargoyle skin rough yet not unpleasant to the touch. "You should've taken me with you to the bog. I could've watched your back and warned you before they attacked. I admit that I was a bit rash the other night by going through a court I don't know much about."

Haven's jaw clenched, but his silence continued to speak truths when he knew she was right.

"But this day isn't forever, Haven," she continued, gently rubbing his arm to soothe him. "The night will come, and if pleasure is the key to unlocking the curse, then be thankful the task is simple." Although, for the first time in her life as a courtesan, a nervous feeling churned in her stomach. It was only because she'd gotten to know Haven first—generally the patron was a stranger and she learned more about them the more they returned to the brothel to visit her.

"Simple to you," he said.

Because Haven still wanted Vivienne, his match…

Rozlyn snipped off a lock of hair and handed it to Haven before he asked for it. After placing the strands into his locket, he trudged toward the full-length mirror hanging inside the wardrobe door and scowled at his wings in the glass. He stepped back, then flapped them, creating a cool gust of wind that caressed her face. After another snap of his wings, he lifted from the floor but only a few hairs before touching back down. As he cracked them again, he remained rooted to the floor this time, his expression strained while not flying upward at all. His shadows seeped out, skimming their dark hands across his wounds—only they didn't heal the least bit.

"This isn't happening," he bellowed, his shadows reeling back inside him.

Rozlyn winced while watching the thin membrane

tear further. "You might want to stop doing that," she called over the boisterous sounds. "Can they not mend on their own if you shift, or do you have a healing salve I can fetch for you in the spell room?"

"I'm not immortal," he muttered, tightening his wings behind him. "And a salve won't do a damn thing. My wings are *fucked*."

"Hmm. Let me see something." Rozlyn folded her arms as she surveyed the Marquis of Shadows' tattered wings in the way she would any fabric. They weren't ruined as he was so quick to believe, and if she mended them like she had the torn dress for Cordelia after a rough and pleasurable night with one of her patrons, his wings would be as good as new. She skirted around him, her smile spreading her cheeks. "I can fix them. Any future flying plans will not be wrecked on my watch."

Haven arched a brow, staring at her as though she'd spoken utter nonsense. "What are you going on about now?"

"Trust me." Rozlyn grabbed him by the hand and tugged him in the direction of the bed. But he stubbornly didn't budge. "Move those big feet of yours, you oaf. I feel as though you'd rather dwell in misery."

He rolled his eyes, yet this time when she pulled him, he allowed her to guide him to the bed. As he sat on the edge of the feathered mattress, Rozlyn studied the ethereal ivory shade of his wings. *A-ha*! She hurried and dug through her satchel until she found the perfect spool of thread that nearly matched.

As she plucked up the needle she'd used earlier, he furrowed his brow. "You're not touching my wings with that."

"How else did you imagine I would fix them?" Angling her head to the side, she held out her things to him and smiled politely. "This is the only way, but if you want, you can stitch them yourself. I'll gladly sit back and wait until you beg for my assistance."

Haven glanced over his shoulder at his wings, but it would, without a doubt, be a failed attempt if he used his own hands. His shadows could perhaps help, but she was certain they wouldn't be as precise or give as much care to the task as she would.

"I suppose they can't get any worse," he relented and leaned forward, allowing her touch to begin.

"I'll do my best," Rozlyn promised while crawling behind him, her eyes fluttering when his pleasant citrusy scent washed over her. As she readied her needle, his wings remained tightly closed behind him. "But you have to open them," she drawled.

His otherworldly wings curled open, and she observed their beauty, regardless of the jagged tears. She glided her fingers over them to get a feel of their surface, the way she would any fabric. They were as soft as velvet, a texture she could run the pads of her fingers across forever.

Haven shivered, and she snapped her hand back,

drawing out of her staring spell. Rozlyn chewed her lip. "I can wait a moment if you need me to."

"No," he said, his voice more strained than usual. "Continue."

As she held the thread beside his right wing, the color was close enough to make the lines resemble veins to blend in with the others. She brought his long, ivory hair over his shoulder, the strands like silk, so it wouldn't get caught in her stitching. Her fingers brushed his neck, and he inhaled sharply.

Rozlyn lifted a layer of delicate membrane and pinched it gently to another section, then pushed the needle in. Haven sat rigid, and his breath barely escaped him, his shadows peeking out every so often. "I'm sorry if this hurts," she murmured.

"It doesn't," he whispered.

Rozlyn blinked. This was the first time he'd held such a light tone when responding to her. Had he liked her touch? Even though he was in love with another woman, that didn't mean someone's touch wouldn't ignite a lustful reaction through them. Skin to skin, nerves against nerves, created pleasure. A warmth bloomed low in her stomach at the thought, but she couldn't focus on such a fleeting emotion—she needed to heal the gargoyle side of Haven.

Tonight they would consummate and hopefully be a step closer to kissing the curse goodbye. No matter that Rozlyn had unknowingly been cursed too, that she was stuck in this tower—she wouldn't want to trap him farther. As grumpy as he was, and even though Madam would tell her she shouldn't, she realized she was starting to consider the Marquis of Shadows a friend.

"What are you planning to do with the coin you earn from your time with me?" Haven asked, his tone unreadable.

It was such a simple answer, a dream Rozlyn had held for years, that she continued to imagine every instance before falling asleep. "Open my own dress shop." She beamed, not missing a beat as she worked the needle through his delicate skin, making sure the stitching was precise so it wouldn't tear when he used his wings again.

"No more courtesan duties?"

"I'm a married woman now, *remember*?" she sang. "A testy sorcerer shared his curse with me, and now I'm bound to him, so it seems I can only dream of the future."

"It sounds like this sorcerer did what was necessary," he said, his deep voice assured.

"Sometimes people are selfish."

"Hmph."

"But," Rozlyn added. "While it might be necessary now, you have to consider what comes after." Her thoughts turned to how Haven wanted revenge on the lord. It was his decision to make, his repercussions to face, not hers.

As she mended the rest of his right wing, he moved too much and she nearly sewed at a tragic angle. "Try not to wiggle like a worm," she reprimanded.

A low growl escaped him, and she tsked, then continued sewing with clarity until the task was complete. Rozlyn tied off the string and studied her art. The stitched lines throughout the membranes gave them a unique design, not perfectly how they were meant to be but perhaps even more beautiful. "There. Good as new." Her heart swelled with pride, her fingers itching to touch them but not only to feel the lines she'd made—to feel *him*.

Rozlyn tamped down her lust as she was taught to do during unnecessary times. Haven peered at his wings and his dark brows rose.

"A thank you would suffice." Rozlyn grinned.

Haven lifted a few red strands of her hair that clung to his arm, and he rubbed them between his fingers. "If your dream is to own a dress shop, do you plan on doing away with your long hair?"

"Unless a certain sorcerer cuts too much and it doesn't grow back"—she winked and stood from the bed, placing her hands on her hips—"then I'm keeping it. If you're not too sore, try out your wings. I can adjust anything if you feel it uncomfortable."

Haven edged to the center of the room and opened and closed his wings. He cracked them once, twice, then his form steadily levitated from the floor.

"No adjustments needed," he said as his feet touched back down. "You did well."

That was the perfect thank you for her.

"Oh, before I forget..." Rozlyn plucked the black knitted socks off the night table. In between reworking a dress, she'd made them while he'd been gone.

"What are those?" he asked as though she were holding a pile of scorpions out to him.

"I wanted to make something different." She smiled, shaking them in front of his face. "And since you like black, you can have them. If you ever want a shirt and trousers made, I'd have to measure you properly for those."

He furrowed his brow, his arms remaining at his sides.

"It's all right—Iseult or Nightshade can have them then." She shrugged and went to place the socks back on the night table when he took them from her hand.

"No, they're mine," he said gruffly.

"That's what I thought." Rozlyn grinned, then leaned into the following question. "So, what happens after tonight?" Yet she knew he would journey straight toward the castle to reunite with Vivienne. Her patrons always returned to their loved ones.

"I still require your hair until the curse completely fades. I'll take one lock at daybreak and another at night, so you'll travel with me across Souldark." His tone didn't sound thrilled about the revelation, but he didn't seem to loath the idea either.

However, Rozlyn's heart sped with giddiness since she wouldn't have to linger in the tower. "We'll protect one another." If something happened to him, the curse could overtake her, and she didn't know precisely what that would mean for her. Perhaps once Haven reached the castle and if he discovered Vivienne and the lord's marriage to be a happy one, then he might give up on revenge.

And if he didn't, it was still his decision to make.

HAVEN

"**P**ack light, then get some sleep," Haven said to Rozlyn and shifted out of his gargoyle form. Beneath his flesh, his wings were whole, not a single throbbing pain, as though they'd never been torn. Because of a bastard princess who took kindness upon him.

"I'll be sure to bring needle and thread." She nodded and knelt beside her satchel, emptying its contents on the floor.

He studied her delicate features for a longer moment than he should've as she sifted through unnecessary items. Then he left and shut the door behind him.

Haven balled his hands into tight fists, still feeling the gentle trail of her soft fingertips against his wings. His shadows stirred, battling against him to reopen the door to touch her, to let her touch him until he groaned.

Tonight they would fuck, but only this once.

He would have his revenge, his match, and Rozlyn would hate him when she discovered she would be sent to Nightshade for the rest of her life. Never would she have the dress shop she so desired in Dawnbreak.

But sacrifices had to be made for the Marquis of Shadows to get what he wanted.

Haven bounded down the tower steps and into the spell room. Iseult stood beside a stack of books on the floor, another four in his skeletal hands. His assistant skated a finger over the spines on the shelf, then placed the books he held near the end.

"You've returned, Marquis," Iseult greeted. "I'm halfway finished putting the books in alphabetical order for you. It will make searching for spell tomes much simpler. Do you need my assistance with anything else?"

Haven's muscles ached, debris clung to him, and he could still smell the stench of the bog in his nose. "A warm bath. Add a couple drops of sandalwood." He scowled. "After sunset, Rozlyn and I will be gone for a handful of days. Maybe more. Once you finish cleaning the tower floors and stairs, you are free to do whatever you want while I'm away. Just make sure the liquid in the cauldrons remains thickened each morning."

Iseult's bony shoulders stiffened, and his jaw parted as he quickly stepped toward Haven. "But, Marquis," he stuttered. "I like to keep busy."

When he'd created Iseult, he hadn't known he would be so compliant, so dutiful, so hardworking. "Then continue taking care of the tower if you'd like, but remember, it's not required this time."

"Thank you, Marquis." Iseult exhaled, the sound one of relief.

"My bath…"

"I'll start it right away." Iseult bowed his head and padded from the room, his robes swishing.

Haven went to the cabinets and rummaged through jars until he found the two he needed. He collected four vials, then filled two of the containers with the yellow and blue liquid before mirroring his movements on the second empty jar.

When night fell, he and Rozlyn would each drink two of the vials to keep their hunger sated and their thirst quenched during the journey. Food and water sources were scarce in most of Souldark. There were exceptions, like Adham's castle and the replenishing food stock in Nightshade's home. The ferryman had Haven's sorcery to thank for his endless supply of wine.

Haven wouldn't be burdened with carrying a satchel—however, he allowed Rozlyn to pack one for her sewing supplies. Not to please her, but in case they were necessary if one of them were wounded. He took the small doll Rozlyn had made off the shelf, along with the spell—both would be used on Adham soon enough.

The edges of Haven's lips curled up as he imagined what it would feel like once the lord's heart was in his fist, then after he stomped on it with his boot.

Haven entered his bathing chamber and inhaled the scent of sandalwood. He made his clothing vanish before sinking down into the warm bath, his shadows seeping out to relax from a long night. His thoughts veered toward Rozlyn, and he would take her outside the tower to fuck her as soon as night fell.

Once Haven finished in the bath, he hadn't found solace in sleep. He'd lain in bed, staring into the darkness, thinking more about fucking Rozlyn than reuniting with Vivienne. But after he and the bastard princess consummated, he could move on, gain composure, and focus on making Souldark his.

A soft knock came at the door. "Haven?" Rozlyn chirped, her voice cheerful. "I told Iseult I would come get you. The sun is setting."

Haven shoved the blankets away from him and snapped his fingers, igniting the flames in his room. His shadows fastened the felt buttons of his shirt before he answered the door.

Rozlyn stood before him wearing a simple black dress

that would make it easier for traveling. And *removing*. "For you." She passed him a flask, and he drank a sip before slipping it into his pocket. "Also this." A lock of hair fell from her hand into his palm, and he added it to the one in his locket.

Her hair was pinned and plaited around her head, and a bright smile spread her dark rouge lips. Irritation washed over him—he knew that smile wasn't because she was going to fuck him but because she was leaving the tower.

"One moment." Haven left the door cracked and slid the doll and death spell into his other trouser pocket. "You can come in now."

Rozlyn pushed open the door, and her doe eyes widened as she looked around the room. "It's just as I imagined. Black."

Haven rolled his eyes and held out two vials toward her while he clasped the others. "Drink these," he instructed.

She hesitated as she brought them close to her face and inspected them.

"They aren't poison or a sleep aid," he continued. "The blue one will keep your hunger away, and the yellow, your thirst."

"Oh!" she chirped. "I wish I had known about these earlier."

When she'd snuck out of the tower… Glowering, he lifted a vial to his lips at the same time Rozlyn did. The blue liquid slid over his tongue, the flavor akin to roast lamb and savory carrots. As the yellow one came next, its taste mirrored that of honey tea.

"Get your satchel and meet me at the entrance," Haven said.

Rozlyn hurried up the stairs, and Haven found Iseult already waiting at the tower entrance.

"Stay safe, Marquis," Iseult said and unlocked the door.

As soon as Rozlyn bounded back down the steps, Iseult opened the entrance and Haven parted the shadow barrier for her.

Once they entered the night and the click of Iseult locking up sounded, Haven's heart unexpectedly thundered inside his chest, slamming against his sternum.

"Where would you like us to go?" she asked softly. "Does it have to be a certain distance outside the tower?"

From what Phoenix had said, consummating should only have to be outside his home. But if he fucked her against its obsidian walls, would that still be considered part of the tower?

Haven felt like a damn fool as Rozlyn waited for him to answer. This was a courtesan who was only fucking him for both coin and the curse. It didn't matter if he was using someone, but he didn't like being used himself. He wanted her to yearn for him, to beg for his length, so it didn't feel as if he were crawling to her as a patron.

He'd been matched young, fucked for the first time

when Vivienne had finally been ready, and he'd never had any trouble burying his cock into her sweet depths. Snapping a throat was simple enough, fucking without someone desperately wanting his cock was another.

Regardless, he needed to consummate this marriage. If they were to get away from the tower, he could take her to the nearest tree, simply unfasten his trousers, hike up her skirts, and thrust his cock into her warm pussy. Moans and groans of spirits drifted through the air, and he scowled. Not once had he and Vivienne ever pleasured one another outdoors. But if it had been last night, he could've easily brought Rozlyn over the edge. But, after a night of overthinking how this would play out, he stood still as the statue he'd become for two years.

Rozlyn's face softened, and she gently placed her palm against his chest. "We have all night, Haven. We can find somewhere else away from the spirits. It can be anywhere outside the tower from what you mentioned. So that means it wouldn't have to even be outdoors," she murmured, her voice soothing. "Pleasure can come later."

Haven's pulse relaxed beneath her touch. She was right about one thing—it didn't have to be outdoors, and he should've realized that sooner. He knew precisely where he would take her for the night. Not uttering another word as his shirt and boots vanished, he drew his shoulders back while his wings burst from his back.

Rozlyn squeaked, her eyes widening, as he lifted her close against his chest and took off into the night sky, his wings snapping with the wind to take them higher.

"You could've warned me!" she shouted over the breeze, her body shaking like a frightened lamb in his arms.

"Consider it foreplay." Haven smirked.

Rozlyn squeezed his neck, and her eyes remained clenched shut as though he would drop her at any moment. He would do far worse to anyone who crossed him, but Rozlyn wasn't his enemy—she never had been—only a maiden of unfortunate parentage who he needed in more ways than one.

With her curvy body pressed against his chest distracting him from observing the world below, he hadn't realized how far they'd traveled until Nightshade's manor came into view. The orange orbs cast a ghoulish glow across the area, and keeping a firm hold around Rozlyn, he descended toward the manor until his feet touched ground.

"You can open your eyes now," Haven said.

Rozlyn cracked open one lid, then the other. "Why are we at Nightshade's?"

"It's the nearest indoor building, and after last night, I don't trust something to not distract us." The will-o'-the-wisps, mainly, but there were other things to worry about in Souldark.

Haven brought Rozlyn to her feet, her breasts brushing his chest, and his cock twitched at her closeness, her sunshine scent.

She stepped back, and Haven released one of his shadows, unlocking the front entrance. He threw open the door and barged into Nightshade's home. The ferryman lay bare on the settee, a different female spirit riding him this time.

"Get the fuck out!" Haven growled.

The female gasped and leapt off Nightshade before snatching up her dress and fleeing through a wall.

The ferryman sat up with a smirk, clearly entertained. "This is my house, you asshole."

"Not for the rest of the night," Haven proclaimed.

"We can go somewhere else," Rozlyn suggested, pressing a hand to Haven's.

"You're lucky I don't tear off your head for not warning me about will-o'-the wisps in the bog."

"Don't act as though you don't know danger lurks everywhere here." Nightshade chuckled while tugging on his trousers. "Besides, I spoke to Phoenix earlier today when I gave him his gondola ride to the gods. He told me precisely *how* you need to finish breaking the curse."

Haven's shadows stormed out from his hands, unfurling and growing in size—a threat. "Out. *Now.*"

"You're being irrational." Rozlyn squeezed his arm.

Nightshade's gaze locked onto her, and his smile turned seductive, his eyes hooded. "It's no issue at all. Breaking the curse helps everyone here. I hope to see you sooner rather than later, Roz."

Haven's nostrils flared at the use of a pet name for a

woman who was still *his*. Once the ferryman sauntered out the front door, he turned to Rozlyn. "We're not fucking in this bastard's sitting room." It would be in Nightshade's bed where the ferryman would know who she belonged to first.

13

ROZLYN

Over the years as a courtesan, Rozlyn had bedded countless men in many ways, many places, and on many pieces of furniture. She hadn't expected the Marquis of Shadows to be almost gentlemanly, in a sense, when it came to finding a proper place to consummate the marriage. And she couldn't help but wonder how he would perform. Would he be soft or rough with his touches, his thrusts? Both styles of the pleasurable act could be pleasing depending on the mood and setting. She'd experienced gratification from various positions and paces—it all could be blissful when done with the right partner.

Haven clasped Rozlyn's hand and led her up a silver

staircase, its rails a swirling ornate design that appeared like rippling water. The walls of the second floor matched the ones in the sitting room, with the same silver leafy vines curving across their surfaces.

The marquis stayed silent, his shoulders squared, his nostrils flaring. The friendship, if that was what one would call it, between him and Nightshade was quite strange. They seemed to help one another in dire circumstances, or at least Nightshade had sent Haven to a sorcerer who'd given advice on the curse. The ferryman hadn't argued about relinquishing his home for the night either. Perhaps Haven was owed for things he'd done for the Souldark Court in the past.

Doors of silver and gold lingered in the hallway, and Rozlyn's heart pounded as she studied Haven's features, the shape of his mouth, the curve of his masculine neck. Besides the first time she'd lost her maidenhead to a patron, not once had she been nervous when preparing for an erotic act. Even when she'd chosen to lose her innocence, Madam had brought her a handsome, younger patron who was well-experienced and would make certain Rozlyn didn't have a horrendous first encounter with the art of pleasure. Madam had told her how the first experience was one that would always be remembered, and if it was regrettably unsatisfying, it could tarnish her views of not only continuing as a courtesan but for future aspects if she ever did desire to leave the brothel and find love. Madam had been accurate in her assumptions.

There were plenty of times when pleasure with patrons wasn't up to par, then she would look back on her first encounter and recall how her orgasm had felt. Cordelia had once told Rozlyn it wasn't only the first time a maiden would remember, but their last, the one that was meant to be forever. However, if one remained a courtesan, there would never be a last time. It would be patron after patron, night after night, lustful encounters that could please for a handful of moments but not forever. That was something Rozlyn had never once minded—perhaps because she knew one day her dream of owning a dress shop could be akin to an eternity of love.

She almost stumbled into Haven when he stopped before a door near the end of the hall. A gondola was etched into the metal, surrounded by moons and suns.

Haven didn't glance back at her as he turned the knob and stepped into the room. When she crossed the threshold, she peered around the large, mostly empty, space. The walls were a deep gray with not a single decoration hung across. A simple bronze wardrobe stood in a corner, and a massive bed with two pillows and white linen sheets rested against the back wall.

Rozlyn approached the wardrobe, curious to see what kind of fabrics it held. As she opened the doors, her shoulders sagged. The inside was barren, just like the landscape and soul of this court.

"Is this a guest room?" she asked as she shut the two doors.

"No," Haven said, drawing back the curtains of the window and staring out at the darkness, "this is Nightshade's bedroom."

"Oh." Rozlyn blinked. She thought about the sex, the wine, the emptiness of the manor, how rowing dead spirits endlessly back and forth across the same lake each day could grow tiresome for someone who didn't love the task. "I believe he's lonely."

"With all the spirits he brings to his home to fuck, I wouldn't say he's lonely," Haven grunted.

The ferryman could still feel that way though. Several of the courtesans who'd worked at the brothel over the years held smiles and empty eyes. Those women generally didn't stay except for the ones who had no other dreams to chase. However, there were the courtesans who found pure joy in making others happy through pleasure, the way Rozlyn had.

Rozlyn snuck another glance at Haven, his back to her as he continued to look out the window. He hadn't made his shirt appear, and her gaze roamed down the beautiful curve of his spine to his backside that his trousers cradled brilliantly, and her pulse hummed. She came to a harsh realization then… It wasn't only lust stirring within her in that moment—she was starting to *like* the Marquis of Shadows, the one rule she couldn't break.

Rozlyn would wave that fickle emotion away. A temporary feeling that could easily be fleeting. Swallowing deeply, she focused on the task that needed to be taken care of tonight. She would perform as she always did, make certain the patron was taken care of and place her thoughts elsewhere. Especially when Haven held affections for another woman, regardless that she was the lady of this court and married to its lord.

"Should we begin?" Rozlyn asked. "Or do you need a few more moments? We have plenty of night remaining."

Haven's hand fell to his side from the wall next to the window, and without a word, he prowled toward her. Her heart galloped, and she ignored the elated feeling. He grasped her wrist and drew her to his chest, his eyes boring into hers. "I won't just bend you over and fuck you quickly. We'll be thorough to make sure this curse doesn't bring us back to the tower. And as your patron, I only have one rule—do not kiss me on the mouth."

Rozlyn nodded. A kiss could be more intimate than anything else. And something he clearly wanted to save for Vivienne. Rozlyn was curious what his lips tasted like, but she would respect his wishes—rarely did she ever kiss patrons anyway. They mostly wanted their cock stroked by her hand or wettened by her tongue or her heat.

If he hiked her skirts up and thrust into her from behind for a few moments, she believed that would be enough to consummate a marriage. But she kept quiet— he was her patron, and a giddy part of her wanted to discover how thorough they could be with one another. A courtesan did always promise to take care of her patron after all.

The line between Haven's brows deepened, and she pressed a hand to his cheek. It didn't matter how she felt about him—he needed to be comfortable. And being intimate with someone when his feelings were for another could easily cause remorse. From time to time, patrons had pretended she were someone else. A grieving widower had imagined Rozlyn as his dead wife—another man thought of her as the woman he was in love with who didn't return his affections. She'd been asked to dress up as a queen, someone a patron would never have. But she'd held the secret of her lineage, of her being a bastard princess who could've been queen, so joy had filled her that she'd been able to secretly satisfy the kind patron's desire.

"You can imagine I'm Vivienne if you need to," she murmured. "I don't mind."

"Silence." Haven unpinned and unplaited her hair until the long, tangled locks fell in thick waves to her ankles.

Rozlyn glided her fingertips over the planes of Haven's chest, down his rippled abdomen to the waistband of his trousers. With nimble fingers, she unfastened the button and dipped her hand inside to free his thick length. His manhood was as large as it had been when she'd seen it in his gargoyle form. A cock that could please any woman—*multiple* times. If he knew how to use it, that was.

As Rozlyn stroked him, his length was as smooth as

marble, his skin like silk. Haven's head fell back, his eyes closed while her hand ventured up and down him, her thumb circling the tip. Was he thinking about Vivienne in that moment? Rozlyn was curious what the lady of the court looked like and how beautiful she was. If she were Haven's perfect sorcery match, Rozlyn believed tales could be written about her.

"Take me in your mouth," Haven growled, his throat bobbing.

Rozlyn obediently sank to her knees, then pulled his trousers to his ankles. Sometimes during these tasks, she imagined herself elsewhere sewing fabrics, but not this instance. Gripping him, she licked his length from base to tip before bringing him fully into her mouth. She massaged his silken skin with her tongue, allowing his cock to drive deeper into her throat.

Her hands glided to his backside, and his hips shifted forward as he thrust into her mouth. The salty taste of his skin was pleasure to her tongue.

"Stop," Haven rasped, extracting his length from her. He grasped her by the arms and drew her from the floor.

Rozlyn peered up at his narrowed eyes. "Was it not good enough for you?" she asked, not once ever having a patron halt her during fellatio. "I can be rougher if you wish."

"It was *too* damn good," Haven said gruffly, his thumb rubbing her arm. "If you keep doing that, I'll fucking come." His fingers reached for the top button at the front of her dress, and he loosened them one by one, then peeled the fabric from her shoulders until her breasts were bare before him. And then her dress pooled to the floor, revealing all of her.

Haven's pupils dilated, the only sign in his expression that gave away his lustful desire. His strong body guided her to the wall near the window, where his mouth so nearly brushed hers. Rozlyn waited for his kiss, to taste the flavor of his lips, his tongue, but he denied her his mouth and slipped down to her jaw instead, nipping and licking. The marquis' heavenly callused hand traveled down her breast, his thumb stroking her nipple before venturing to her core, his palm punishingly and exquisitely pressing against her pearl.

"Oh!" Rozlyn gasped. Her eyelids fluttered when he dipped two fingers inside her heat while his palm moved deftly against her. A long moan escaped her as she arched into him and rode his hand.

"Put your hands on the wall," Haven demanded and turned her around, his hard cock glided up and down her backside, her core. Rozlyn's body trembled, anxiously awaiting him to fill her as he grasped her breasts, kneading them while his lips expertly tasted the crook of her neck and down her shoulder.

"You come when I say," he ground out, then slid his cock inside her with one hard thrust, and her breath hitched.

Haven's hands dug into her hips, and he moved his

lower half in a way that was utterly spellbinding. Another arm circled her waist—one of his shadows. Her lips parted as it skimmed down to her center, then pushed her clit and she could barely find breath from the intoxicating touch.

"The bed. Ride me," Haven demanded, then pulled out of her. She nearly whimpered at the loss of his cock.

He lifted her as though she weighed nothing and brought her down to straddle him on the bed. Rozlyn clasped his shoulders and sank down on him when he took a nipple into his mouth, his hand fisting her hair. She rolled her hips into his, her pace turning harder, faster, the groans and growls becoming more frequent from him while she put everything into her art form.

"Come," he ordered.

Haven's fingers yanked on her hair in a delicious way. The friction in her core grew ravenous as the exquisite feeling drew closer, until a pleasureful wave crashed into her, her body quaking. She cried from the orgasm alight within her, akin to a thousand shooting stars.

"Good girl." Haven smirked. Then he peeled Rozlyn from him and placed her on her hands and knees. The marquis moved off the bed and stood behind her on the floor, wrapping her hair around his hand. He was only gone momentarily before slamming into her, her backside meeting him thrust for thrust. Her breasts bounced as he pulled her hair, fully burying himself in her and shouting, "Fuck!" And then again, but slower, raspier. *"Fuck."*

Rozlyn fell to the bed when he pulled out of her, her head collapsing against a velvet pillow. Haven didn't move, only stared down at her, his jaw clenched, his chest heaving.

Neither said a word, until she remembered something. She hurried from the bed and opened her satchel to retrieve her tonic. She drank two bitter swallows as Haven drew on his trousers. His slitted gaze traveled down her bare form, lingering on her breasts. "Get dressed, then sleep. We'll stay here until morning to see if it worked," he said.

She hadn't expected that they would sleep there, but she nodded and put on her dress before laying on the bed. Unless he requested more pleasure from her, the consummation was the end of it.

Haven drank from his flask and left a large gap between them when he sank onto the bed—as though they'd never been intimate.

The way of a patron and his courtesan.

14

HAVEN

Soft, steady breaths escaped Rozlyn's shapely lips as she slumbered beside Haven. He'd managed to slip briefly into sleep after having not slept well during the day. And perhaps Rozlyn had struggled with the same issue before they'd left the tower since she'd fallen asleep almost as soon as she'd crawled into bed. He looked toward the window, where darkness still reigned. The sun would rise at any moment, so if they remained at Nightshade's manner, he wanted to leave as soon as possible. Two years was fucking long enough to wait.

Haven's original plan had been to come into Nightshade's room, fuck Rozlyn on the ferryman's bed, and be finished in mere moments. But when the words *should we begin* left her plump lips, he hadn't wanted sex to be fast and done with. He hadn't fucked anyone in two years and he'd deserved an orgasm that would satisfy him.

The marquis hadn't desired to only please himself, but *her*. How many times had Rozlyn been rewarded as a courtesan when pricks came to her requesting only their lengths be sucked or a quick cock to a warm pussy? As her hot mouth so brilliantly catered to Haven's cock with such precision and focus, he'd only thought of her, not Vivienne. He'd tried to imagine Vivienne's tongue swirling up his length, but he fucking couldn't. And then he'd wanted to feel Rozlyn's slick folds with his fingers, and it hadn't only been him, his shadows had demanded to touch her too.

Sex with Vivienne had been damn good, but with Rozlyn, it was utterly gratifying. More pleasurable. He hadn't known how refreshing a courtesan could be. But that didn't matter—it was only lust. His match was what he needed, and after the night spent with Rozlyn, it would make him and Vivienne even. Haven wouldn't regret not thinking of her when fucking Rozlyn. As Vivienne was riding Adham to orgasm, Haven knew good and well that she wasn't thinking of him.

Pathetic.

As temptation got the best of him, Haven cast a glance at Rozlyn, her parted lips, the swells of her breasts peeking out from the neckline of her dress. If she'd remained unclothed, he knew he would've given in and taken her again, fucked her until they were lying in tangled ruins. He regretted not tasting her sweet pussy. And her mouth … but he wouldn't garner the flavor of her lips. For the match's sake.

Haven's gaze lingered on her form, and he wanted to curve his body around hers. He tightened his fists, then stood from the bed, knowing he would wake her for pleasure if he stayed there.

At Nightshade's bedroom window, he waited for the sun to rise. Mist rolled beneath the orange orbs, and stars flecked the sky like sparkling jewels. The bastard had known better than to return. Haven didn't want the ferryman looking at her again. But Nightshade would eventually see her every day… Because of the bargain.

Once Rozlyn roused from sleep, what would he say to her? He couldn't admit that she would be given to the ferryman instead of returning to open her dress shop.

Haven white-knuckled the window sill—he didn't owe a courtesan a damn thing. She'd willingly come to Haven, and while under his contract, he had the right to bargain her. Nightshade was who she would have to barter with for freedom, but deep down in his savage heart, he knew the ferryman would ensnare her forever because of her royal lineage. A bargain was a bargain, and even if Haven wanted to go back on the arrangement, Nightshade would deny him. There was nothing the immortal wanted more than power, and Rozlyn would give him that.

It wouldn't matter to him how many men Rozlyn had fucked either since the ferryman had pleasured countless more. Perhaps they were a match in their own right. A bastard princess and a bastard half-god whose parents hadn't chosen to keep them.

Haven gritted his teeth as he imagined Nightshade yanking on Rozlyn's hair as he thrust into her from behind, the way Haven had. His blood boiled, his heartbeat raging, and he torched the thought before it consumed him.

"The sun is rising." Rozlyn yawned.

Morning light spilled through the window, and he'd been caught too much inside his own head to take fucking notice of the thing that truly mattered.

He turned to face Rozlyn, watching as she stretched her arms. Her breasts lifted higher, and he bit the inside of his cheek until he tasted metal and looked back out the window. *One fuck. That is all that will ever happen between us. No more.*

Haven opened his locket to see if there was a possibility he wouldn't need Rozlyn's hair, that maybe he could send her back to the tower so he wouldn't be tempted to take her again. But the lock of hair from the day before had turned gold, while the more recent one was still ruby red. A part of him was pleased that he still needed her.

Fabric rustled, and Haven found Rozlyn digging into her satchel and fishing out a pair of scissors. Though he hadn't demanded it of her yet, she snipped a piece of her hair, then placed it into his palm with a smile. "Here."

Haven furrowed his brow as he studied her bright expression. Why was she smiling at him? She'd never once had a joyous expression when it came to cutting her hair. It hadn't mattered if it grew back afterward. Being free from the tower must've made the small sacrifice worthwhile for her.

He snapped his locket shut. "Gather your things. We're leaving."

"How far is the castle from here?" she asked as she slipped her satchel's strap over her head.

"Two or three days. I won't be flying the entire way, so prepare yourself for a long walk when instructed. Do as I say and don't do anything foolish," Haven said, holding her gaze.

Rozlyn bounced as she struggled to pull her second boot on. "Being curious isn't always foolish."

Haven rolled his eyes. He noticed a long tendril of hair hung near her eye, and he caught himself when he lifted his hand to brush it behind her ear. "Tie your hair back up and meet me downstairs."

Rozlyn gathered the pins that had fallen on the floor the night before. She appeared unfazed that they'd fucked, but why would she? The sun was shining and they weren't trapped in the tower.

Even though Haven's thirst had subsided, he drank from his flask as he descended the stairs. The burn was exactly what he needed to push away the memories of the night before.

Now that it was dawn, Nightshade would be hard at work. By now, he was already at his gondola, tediously rowing spirits across the lake.

A few moments later, Rozlyn met Haven near the porch, her scarlet hair drawn back, revealing her round face. The sun's rays highlighted her soft and delicate features more than ever.

"Hold onto me as you did yesterday," Haven instructed. He told himself it was so he could use his hands if necessary, but selfishly, it was to have her body flush with his, even if he wouldn't allow it to lead to fucking.

"Let's see if I get used to the nightmare of falling to my death," she said as she wrapped her arms around him, then circled his hips with her legs.

"Perhaps if you kept your eyes open," Haven drawled. But he had to admit she'd faced her fears well when he'd flown her the prior night. She hadn't argued or complained.

As Rozlyn adjusted her hold on him, her breasts rubbing his chest, he swallowed deeply. His hands veered down to her backside to hold her steady, and he released the gargoyle part of him. With one crack of his wings, he took off into the cloudy sky.

In the distance, the mist grew thicker, making it harder for him to see what rested before them. Rozlyn trembled, but she kept quiet, taking everything in stride. As he thought about it, Rozlyn was the only woman he'd ever carried. Not once had Vivienne flown in his arms across this court, only beside him in her raven form. He'd never asked her, even though he'd wanted to fuck in the air a time or two.

For hours, Haven soared Rozlyn past flat landscape and over several dried-up lakes. He only took a break here and there so they could stretch their muscles. Rozlyn's stitching had worked well on his wings as though they'd never been torn. As they traveled through heavy mist, his vision straining, a foul stench pierced the air, far bolder than the bog had been.

"It smells like rotten meat," Rozlyn said, burying her nose into his shoulder.

"This is pleasant compared to some of the places further west." He smirked.

A soft bite came at his shoulder, and he fought a smile. Before he could say anything, thunder rumbled and lightning snaked across the sky.

Fuck! They were still a good distance from the abandoned cottage he planned to rest in. Lightning illuminated the sky again in pinks and oranges. Rozlyn gripped him tighter and Haven wound his arms around her waist. The gods' power was something Haven's sorcery was no match against.

"Should we go down?" Rozlyn shouted over another boom of thunder.

Haven descended, searching for shelter. In the distance, a manor slipped into view. He'd never spent the night in it before, but he'd been inside on one occasion when he was younger. The sorceress who'd once lived there had embedded parts of her spirit into the walls. Remnants of her spelled objects lingered, making the visit unpredictable and potentially dangerous. The stay would be much smoother than a storm in Souldark though.

He soared toward the manor, finding it nowhere near as lush as the place where he generally stayed. All of the windows were cracked, broken, or completely gone. Paint chipped from the green shutters that still managed to cling to the siding, and the roof had a gaping hole. The porch was empty, the gardens full of rows of dead bushes.

Droplets of rain began to fall from the sky just before he landed near the door. "We'll sleep here for the night," he announced.

Rozlyn slid from Haven's body, and he released his shadows to put barriers across the windows and roof. As Haven and Rozlyn stood beneath the porch, the sky opened and heavy rain poured from its gray depths. He ignored the storm and unlocked the door with his shadow, then stepped over the threshold first so he could monitor and locate any corrupt sorcery. The manor looked just as it had when he went inside years ago.

Rozlyn peered around the home, her mouth agape, and her doe eyes shining. "Everything is upside down in here. I love it!" Cups, jars, books, the table—anything and everything. Above them, various-sized jars were stuck to the ceiling's entirety.

"Love it?" He arched a brow. It looked like a clustered fucking disaster.

"Yes!" she chirped.

"It used to belong to a sorceress of the Shaderain Court." He shrugged. "It was rumored she was mad and altered animals using her spelled objects. A chicken with the legs of a goat and the body of a mule, for one. She'd tried it on people too, including a young prince, which was one of the many reasons why she was shunned from the court. A bit boorish to use one's sorcery in that way if you ask me."

Rozlyn gasped. "That's positively frightening, especially if it were my head being swapped with that of a goat! Would my mind be inside the goat, or would the goat's mind be mine?"

"That all depends on what the sorcery wielder chooses. Would you like me to try?" He lifted a hand.

"No! And that better have been a jest."

"I never jest." Haven smirked. "Now, come on."

Rozlyn followed him down the hall where paintings of mutilated animals hung upside down. As they reached a dusty staircase, she asked, "What is the Souldark village like where the lord lives?"

"Cottages, markets, a castle. But once a sorcerer or sorceress takes a home in the village, they aren't allowed to leave." It was one of the reasons Haven had never chosen to live there when Adham offered him a cottage. *Before* the lord had fucked Vivienne. Now he wondered if the offer was made simply so Vivienne would be closer.

Rozlyn tilted her head. "Why?"

"Because *the lord* says so," Haven grumbled when they reached the top of the stairs. It was a tradition that had been passed down through the generations. Supposedly it kept the court safer, but to Haven it was a way to keep the villagers tamed.

"Is he a good man?" Rozlyn placed a palm over Haven's mouth as he scowled. "Besides the situation that happened with Vivienne."

"You mean besides him *fucking* my match," Haven said after removing Rozlyn's dainty hand from his lips.

"Yes, that." Rozlyn winced.

Haven thought about his journeys to the Souldark Castle over the years. He'd been eleven when he first met the twenty-one-year-old lord. Adham had always been demanding of the villagers, but he hadn't been cruel, at least not to those surrounding his castle. The rest of Souldark he didn't give a fuck about and left it for Nightshade to deal with. Spirits didn't matter to the lord in the least—it was just something he'd inherited when his father died.

"He's a fucking selfish bastard who shouldn't be in charge of any court," Haven spat.

"And you wouldn't be selfish if you were a lord?" Rozlyn asked, cocking her head.

He arched a brow. "I'm always a selfish bastard, and I don't pretend otherwise."

Haven knew exactly what he was doing, and he would never go back on his plan. A weak-minded sorcerer wouldn't be the perfect match for anyone. As for the court, he only wanted it to impress Vivienne.

Haven's thumb ring warmed, and he looked down, watching as it changed from black to white. Haven wasn't a fortune teller by any means, but he assumed that meant the remnants were awakening. Something not quite dead and not quite alive. He would create a spelled barrier in a room to keep the fuckers out.

Swishing echoed from behind the closed doors in the hallway, all but one near the end, and his ring darkened as they approached. He threw it open, and a set of stairs ascended before him that led to the attic.

Rozlyn clenched her dagger, not a hint of fear in her eyes.

A dagger would do nothing against this magic. But he would make damned sure his sorcery did.

15

ROZLYN

The attic stairs creaked beneath Rozlyn's feet as she padded up the wooden steps behind Haven, her bronze dagger tight in her grip. A blade might not work against magic, but if a spirit could be pleasured by Nightshade, then she could still surely stab one, even if it didn't kill them. Being taken off guard would give enough time for Haven to release his sorcery on one.

Orange candles burning in golden sconces along the walls, papered in cerulean willow trees, hung upside down like everything else in this manor. Yellow flames with black centers licked across the wicks, the glow casting shadowy images of what looked to be skeletal stags dancing, the wax remaining in place as it had in Haven's tower.

When they reached the top of the stairs, Haven pressed a palm and an ear against the door, seeming to be listening and feeling for sorcery.

Rozlyn craned her neck, and the only sounds she could hear were her own breath accompanied by Haven's. "The swishing stopped," she whispered.

"I don't trust noises that suddenly disappear," Haven said, his shadows crawling down the walls and door, claws slipping out from their inky hands, before seeping through them.

Like a clock, the moments ticked by inside Rozlyn's head until Haven nodded to himself and opened the door. He slipped inside while holding out a hand, motioning with a finger for her to come.

Rozlyn stepped into a large attic, the room hexagonal in shape. Three chandeliers were planted on the floor, yet in a straight position as though they were dangling from the ceiling. Peeling maroon wallpaper of upside-down white bears covered every inch, including above them. The furniture wasn't on the floor but on the ceiling, all bright colors. A magenta settee, yellow chaise, lime green table, two orange chairs, a writing desk, and a lavender wool rug. Shelves decorated the walls with glass figurines of dancing women, each standing in the reversed position by their heads.

The floor and walls shook, the glass figurines vibrating yet not collapsing to the floor. Rozlyn pulled

Haven by the arm in case the settee above them decided to come crashing down. His shadows curled from his hands just as a ruby apparition seeped from the floor, its shape like an octopus. A red tentacle lashed forward and wrapped around Haven's wrist, and Rozlyn sliced through it. Before she could stab into the creature again, Haven's shadow had already cut through the head. The top portion slid to the floor, and the creature convulsed, both parts disappearing back to the depths from which they'd come.

"What kind of magic is *that*?" Rozlyn asked, inspecting Haven's wrist where a red mark rested, but the injury wasn't bad enough to need a healing salve.

"They are old remnants of spelled objects that have taken on a life of their own. Some hold parts of the sorceress' spirit that was divided throughout the manor. They should've remained hidden because they will now have to discover what I can do," Haven growled. He then opened a closet door in the middle of the far wall and nudged her inside. "Stay put."

Haven shut the door before she could argue, and she was left to her defenses, surrounded by darkness. He spoke low words on the other side of her door, words that sounded as though they were in another language. Swishing stirred once more, the volume increasing, the noise louder than anything she'd ever heard, to the point where she couldn't hear anything else. She didn't cover her ears though, only attempted to continue listening as she winced.

Silence followed, long and never-ending. Time ticked and ticked and *ticked*. Fear pulsed through Rozlyn when not even Haven's boots made a creak against the wooden planks.

She slowly opened the door, surveying the empty attic. No sign of Haven. Her heart hammered. The Marquis of Shadows would tell her to obey him and hover in the closet, but if something had happened to him, or if he needed her, she couldn't linger behind like a weak animal. The other door to the stairs was drawn wide, and she stepped forward to hurry down them to the next floor just as Haven entered at the bottom. His fiery gaze latched onto hers, fury swirling in his pale eyes.

"Can you ever obey?" he snapped, his feet stomping against the steps toward her.

"You were taking too long!" she hissed. "And then you were gone from the room! I told you I would watch your back. Not cower in a corner of a dark closet, where I couldn't see anything, I might add!"

"I know what I'm doing," he said as he towered above her, his chest heaving.

"Did you forget that you were wounded a moment ago?" she pointed out, jabbing him in his sternum.

"I'll live, won't I?"

She pursed her lips. "Unless there is a delayed reaction and your hands fall off, then the poison travels to your heart and squeezes the organ to death."

Haven stared at her, unblinking. "That's absurd."

When moans reverberated beneath them, and shadowy scarlet heads resembling nefarious sea creatures peaked through the floor, he ground out, "Closet. Now."

Rozlyn didn't question him and fled inside with Haven behind her. He shut them into the darkness, but a moment later, orange orbs flickered above them, bobbing just like the ones outside Nightshade's manor.

Haven lifted his hand, making a myriad of different shapes. A triangle. Circle. Some sort of squiggles as though he were writing a letter. The closet was much tinier with him standing beside her, and if she were as claustrophobic as her friend Cordelia, she might've panicked in the corner.

Once Haven's hand fell back to his side, he calmly drew in a breath. "The fuckers are gone, but we'll stay in here until dawn. There were more remnants than I'd expected. The last time I was here as a boy, there had barely been any."

"They must like me then," she jested.

"Hmph."

"I'm fine with staying in here though," she said as she watched the orbs float above them. "Did you create the ones at Nightshade's manor too?"

"I did." He frowned, flexing his hands at his sides.

She thought about the two encounters she'd witnessed between the two men. Haven's mood wasn't the least bit cheerful around him, more so on edge each time. "But you seem to hate him."

His eyebrow lifted. "I don't hate the fucker."

Rozlyn blinked. It was a very strange friendship indeed. However, if he didn't consider the ferryman an enemy, then she wondered how he treated those who were. *Oh yes, the labyrinth…*

Perhaps she was used to how she and the other courtesans interacted, never once having an argument with any of them. She knew some might perceive her as a doormat, yet she just preferred to get along. But she had seen the other girls get into nasty spats at times—hair pulling, slaps, a drink to the face. Envy over when a wealthy client chose one courtesan over the other. A few would act as though nothing had happened while others held grudges that never went away.

"Well, I think Nightshade—" A nip, like a pinch, came at her neck and she clamped her hand against flesh. "Something bit me!" she shrieked.

"Stop mentioning Nightshade and my shadows won't do it again," he muttered. A hint of jealousy lingered in his voice. Did he think she wanted to be the ferryman's courtesan?

"Fine," she relented. "But just so you know, I'd rather be trapped in this closet with you over drinking a glass of wine in *his name I shall not say's* manor."

"Good." Haven backed into the wall and sank down onto the floor, his large body taking up most of the space.

One of her feet rested beside the door and another

between his legs, leaving her nowhere to really go. She placed her hands on her hips and tilted her head to the side. "What am I supposed to do? Stand the entire night? Or, better yet, *sleep* while standing?"

Haven shrugged, his expression neutral. "You can."

He desperately needed to work on how to interact with people, but she found him rather endearing in his own way. "Make room, sorcerer," Rozlyn huffed and settled between his legs, then leaned against his firm chest.

She could feel the steady thump of his heart against her back, and now that everything had calmed down inside the house, she could do nothing but think. Think about the night before. The Marquis of Shadows' touches, the way he made her moan with his fingers and cock. How his tongue and lips had felt like silk against her throat. As his warmth cocooned her, she would take the torture of yearning for his touches over standing the whole night.

Haven surprised her when he was the first to speak. "How did you end up in a brothel anyway?" It came as a surprise that he wanted to learn more about her, but that was what friends would do.

Rozlyn released a breath, recalling her grim childhood, something she chose to keep at the bottom of an abundance of happy things. When she was younger, even after discovering Madam and the woman's brothel, the memories had plagued her until she allowed herself to be loved. Rozlyn had thought either Madam would use her for her own purposes the way her mother had, or would only care for her so long before throwing her back to the streets.

"My mother was madly in love with my father, the king of Dawnbreak—as you know," Rozlyn murmured. "She would always go on about how one day he would finally ask her to be his wife, that she would live in his palace and have so many riches that she would never have to worry. Only her, never me. The king was already married at the time, you see, and my mother was his mistress. When I was a child, he would come to our meager home for pleasure from my mother while I sewed in another room. He never told me hello, never once gave me a hug or a smile. My mother only saw me as the key to becoming his wife, his queen, and when he no longer came around, she abandoned me. I was nine years old, left to fend for myself. Which, back then, I didn't know how to do. The madam of a brothel found me wandering the streets in search of my mother and took me in."

"And she forced you to work for her?" he said between gritted teeth, his arm circling her waist as he sat straighter. "At nine years old?"

"No!" she whisper-shouted. "I chose that path when I was older. The courtesans kept me shielded, protected me, and Madam trained me to fight in case I ever needed to defend myself again. She may not be my blood, but I consider her my mother. I promised myself the one thing

I would never do was fall in love and become someone's mistress, even though a courtesan is in a sense, regardless of her feelings."

Haven remained quiet for several heartbeats. "I still can't believe you wouldn't choose to be a fucking princess, especially since you're the first heir to the throne, bastard or not. I don't know anyone who would turn down power, wealth, and beauty to live as a courtesan," he said, incredulous.

"It seems you don't know a lot of people." Rozlyn tsked. "A courtesan can have all those things. So can a dressmaker. But if I never have any of those things, it doesn't make a difference." She turned in his arms and lifted his chin. "When it comes to beauty, I'm not a hideous beast, and even if I was, would it matter?"

"You know what I mean," he said. "Pampered with powders and fine clothing. You could fashion your hair any way you desired."

"I like my hair this long, *Haven*," Rozlyn drawled, wanting desperately to kiss him, to feel his lips against hers. But she would respect his wishes—no kisses. "And if I was inside the palace walls, it would continue to remain so."

"I liked the feel of your hair in my hands last night," he said, his tone gruff, his warm breath mingling with hers.

Heat pooled low in her belly, and her voice came out breathy as she spoke, "If you require my assistance, all you have to do is ask." Even if he wasn't her patron, and it wasn't for the curse, she would want to find pleasure with him a second time. But she knew that would only make her want to do it again and again.

"Go to sleep," he rasped, yet his arm remained around her waist, and she relaxed against his comforting chest.

Rozlyn closed her eyes and pretended as if she were in her dress shop with fabrics of every color and texture, reminding herself that a courtesan was never supposed to fall in love.

HAVEN

Rozlyn rolled onto her side, her soft lips so very near to brushing Haven's chest. Her breath came out slow and even as she slept, and he kept his arm folded around her waist. It was only to anchor her to him if any of the dark remnants broke through his sorcery. But he was confident that nothing could get past it.

Throughout the rest of the night, Haven drifted into dark dreams and woke several times, but it was enough to keep him clear-headed on the journey. He'd grown used to not getting proper sleep, used to his thoughts and rage keeping him up at all hours. Even in his gargoyle state, he'd rarely slept, and at night, when he broke free of his marble cage, he'd been determined to find a way to rid himself of the fucking curse.

But the past few times he'd closed his eyes, Rozlyn was pressed against his chest. And it was her who drove his thoughts.

Beneath the eerie orange glow of the orbs, Haven peered down at his cuff and found that it had faded a little. Rozlyn's appeared the same. The consummation had worked wonders, and soon, the binding objects wouldn't be on their wrists at all. When they vanished, he would have to deliver Rozlyn to Nightshade's manor… *Fuck him.*

Rozlyn exhaled slowly, drawing his attention back to her face. She was far too trusting—a weakness. What she hadn't realized was Haven didn't need to bring them into this closet at all. He could've simply kept them in the larger part of the attic that he'd also warded, where they could've slept farther apart. But he'd been a selfish bastard, wanting her body against his, even if it was torture for him. And it had been. He could only imagine what it would be like to lick his tongue up her wet pussy. At least once. It was a regret that would burden him—he should've done it the night they'd consummated. Yet he didn't only want to fuck her core with his tongue—he wanted her mouth back around his cock until he spilled himself inside her so he could watch her expression as she swallowed his cum.

Fuck.

Haven had tortured himself long enough, and it was

time they left. They'd gotten enough rest and his shadows informed him that the storm had stopped hours ago. If he remained there, he would be too tempted to whisper in Rozlyn's ear and ask if she wanted to be fucked again. And he knew her answer would undoubtedly be *yes*. There was no more time to waste though.

Lifting his hand to the wall, he released his shadows to make certain the remnants weren't lurking about, waiting in dark crevices. When his shadows slipped back inside him, it was almost dawn and clear to leave—the remnants hadn't dared to show themselves again. Without a doubt, they feared what Haven could do to them if they got near Rozlyn.

If it hadn't been for coin or believing the curse would turn her to stone, would Rozlyn have already attempted to run away? Even though Haven would return to stone without her hair, Rozlyn wouldn't become a marble gargoyle outside the tower. He'd lied to her. But lies were necessary to keep one obedient. He knew Vivienne well, and she would've left him to his own devices if she'd uncovered the truth. Something about Rozlyn made him believe she wouldn't.

"Get up," Haven said, gently shaking her shoulder. "The storm's over and we need to leave."

Rozlyn made another soft noise and yawned, her back rising against his chest. He took a harsh swallow as she turned to face him, his arm still bound around her.

"Is it already morning?" she asked as she stood and

stretched her arms.

Haven studied her curves for far too long before he answered, "Almost." He waved a hand, needing to distance himself for a moment, and the closet door opened.

"I have your back." Rozlyn retrieved her dagger, and her concerned stare met his. It was a look he hadn't seen from a woman in a very long time. She *cared* about him, considered him a *friend*.

His chest unreasonably tightened. That would change nothing. Not his revenge. And not her outcome in the end.

Rozlyn stepped into the attic room while he pushed up from the floor, stretching his numb legs. Haven inspected the area, his piercing gaze boring into the walls, before nodding. She didn't wait for him to lead her—instead, she brushed ahead of him down the staircase and into the hall, her gaze sweeping the walls and the path. He couldn't tell whether she was brave or foolish, but there was nothing here she needed to fear at the moment.

The manor stayed quiet as they slipped outside into the light mist, the sun rising somewhere behind the overcast sky. Pools of water lingered across the land of hardened dirt from the heavy storm. Rozlyn snipped off a tendril of hair, and Haven replaced the golden one in his locket.

After relieving themselves near the manor, Rozlyn drew a cookie from a small silk sack in her satchel.

She bit into the dessert with a delicate sigh as he arched a brow and inhaled a bit of cinnamon. "Why are you eating?" Haven grunted. "It's unnecessary."

"You don't have to drink your liquor, yet you have." Rozlyn winked. "I was in the mood for something sweet." She broke the cookie in half and held the unbitten piece in front of his face. "Here."

He didn't part his lips for her, only studied the cookie and its colorful chunks. "You made this?" he inquired.

"Your kitchen allows one to get creative with their food. So I did." She smiled brighter and nudged the cookie against his lips. "One bite."

Haven furrowed his brow but opened his mouth and bit into the dessert, mostly so he could feel her fingertips against his lips. An overly sweetened blend of sugar and fruits slid against his tongue. Not entirely awful, but something he wouldn't have chosen for himself. "Too sweet," he said as he chewed.

"Ah, so you like your desserts more bitter." She pressed her hand back into the silk bag and revealed a square piece of dark chocolate. "I had guessed your tastes already and brought you something along too."

Haven narrowed his eyes—he didn't need her to care about him, to know the exact things he enjoyed eating. And while he wanted to tell her he loathed those sweets, that she was wrong, he took the chocolate she now offered him and chewed. Of course it was fucking delicious.

"And I was right." She grinned, stuffing the sack back into her satchel. "If you want another, I have more."

"We've wasted enough time." Haven released his wings and placed one of Rozlyn's arms around his neck, then folded his hands over her backside as she held onto him.

He took off through the mist, his wings cracking like thunder against the strong gust of wind. Rozlyn's trembles remained at a minimum compared to the prior times. The stench wasn't as strong as the prior day, and he flew them for a couple of hours before descending.

He didn't need one of Adham's spies reporting that the Marquis of Shadows was heading toward the castle. It wouldn't be hard to tell who a winged gargoyle was, and while some might believe Haven was visiting, that wouldn't be the case with Adham. He would know it was for revenge and Haven wanted to arrive with no warning at all.

A forest of dead trees appeared through the mist as he drew closer. "We'll travel on foot from here on out," Haven said.

"I like the sound of that much better," Rozlyn shouted over the wind, cracking one eye open.

"If you're afraid of boats, then you might want to prepare yourself," he grumbled.

"I love boats!" she chirped, her body no longer trembling.

Haven rolled his eyes, but he found himself fighting a

smile. He frowned at that—nothing she did or said should've been the least bit adorable. Once Vivienne begged for Haven to bed her, any thoughts and temptations he'd had would end.

As he touched down on rocky ground, Rozlyn left his grasp and held onto his arm to steady herself against the uneven terrain. He drew his gargoyle form back inside himself and waved a hand in the air for his shirt and boots to cloak him.

Haven walked beside Rozlyn at a brisk pace through the forest of dead trees, her smaller legs struggling to keep up, yet she didn't complain. Through the light mist, not a single thing—living or dead—milled about. He kept his attention trained on the tops of the trees as well as their surroundings when he recalled the fucking will-o'-the-wisps slinking out from the bog.

They continued walking south and the ground became rockier until they broke through the narrow trees. There, a murky green lake produced a foul sulfuric odor. A squishing sound filled the air as the water rippled.

"This is *pleasant*," Rozlyn drawled, cupping her nose and mouth. "I hope you don't mean for us to swim across it."

Haven's stare fixed on a small white boat gliding across the water in their direction, a young dark-haired sorcerer rowing the oars, his back facing them. "No," he said. "I told you we were taking a boat."

Haven stepped back with Rozlyn into the shadows of

the trees and waited for the boat to dock. As the man knelt to rope it, Haven grasped Rozlyn's hand and led her across the dock.

"That's not necessary," Haven said, his shadows unfastening the rope. He stepped into the boat with Rozlyn in his arms just as the man whirled to face them.

"Get out, you bastards!" he shouted, drawing out a spelled crystal.

Haven cocked his head, his shadows pouring out of him, shaping into blades and swirling closer to the man. "Now, is that any way to speak in front of a lady?"

Rozlyn scoffed. "As if you don't have a filthier mouth."

The man froze, then he bowed his head and dropped to one knee. "Marquis of Shadows, I didn't realize it was you. You may use my boat for however long you wish."

"If you mention I was here," Haven said slowly, his words promising punishment. "My shadows will slice you apart so I can mount the pieces inside my tower."

"I vow I will do no such thing," he stuttered, his eyes remaining trained on the wooden dock.

"Good." Haven sat on the boat seat and patted the spot beside him for Rozlyn. She blinked and sank down next to him as his shadows clasped the oars and rowed them away from the dock.

"Will you really do that?" Rozlyn asked.

"I think you know the answer."

She cocked her head and folded her arms. "A

forgetting spell would make situations like that less bloody."

Haven arched a brow and smirked. "Such simple advice. It's a wonder I never thought of that."

"Glad you'll consider it then." She smiled, resting her satchel on the boat floor as he rolled his eyes.

When the boat drifted farther from the land, the foul odor dissipated, replaced by the scent of rain. The murky water became crystal clear, but that only made the situation worse for travelers.

"Are those bodies below us?" Rozlyn gasped.

"Yes," Haven said, peering over the side of the boat as gray spirits churned around one another, their eyes wide, unable to blink any longer. "Once a spirit's energy has been completely snuffed out by Souldark's creatures, they wander to this lake and remain here."

"No one can help them?"

"They should've helped themselves." It wasn't as if Nightshade's job was a secret—all they had to do was find him. Perhaps barter with him if needed.

"Maybe if—" Two hands clamped down on the edge of the boat, then tugged it downward. Rozlyn and Haven lurched sideways, and his shadows slammed into the spirit, knocking it back into the water. Another seized Rozlyn's wrist before yanking her out of the boat, the lake swallowing her screech.

Haven's pulse raced as he jerked up from his seat, his blood pumping with fury. He shoved his shadows deep into the water, knowing they could glide much faster within the lake than he could. They searched through the collection of entwined bodies, pushed away their reaches, until a writhing light drew their attention, the maiden's hair as red as blood. His shadows latched onto Rozlyn— another sliced through the spirit clutching onto her until it released her. Haven's shadows held her closely, and she relaxed into them as they pulled her back up into his awaiting grasp. He held her firmly against his chest while a rack of coughs left her, her shoulders trembling.

"Well, that wasn't the bath I would've chosen," Rozlyn croaked.

"Don't look at them again," he ground out. "You'll only tempt them to snatch you."

She turned in his arms and cupped his face, then pressed her lips to his cheek. "Thank you for not letting me drown."

"I still need you alive," he said as his fingers brushed the skin where her lips had been.

17

ROZLYN

Light sprinkles fell from the sky, and Haven cursed at them. As though the marquis' sorcery had won in his favor against the gods, the rain ceased. It wouldn't have mattered much if the rain had poured down harder, at least for Rozlyn since she was soaked to the bone after being dragged out of the boat and below the lake's surface by a spirit. She could still feel the rail-thin fingers clamped around her shoulders, could still see the other unblinking bodies below the surface, reaching to take her for their own. To where? It could've only been to her death. And would they have trapped her soul down there too? She shuddered at the thought.

It had only taken Haven's shadows brief moments to

free her from the spirit's clutches, and as soon as those comforting inky hands had grasped her, she'd felt safe. Her and Haven's cuffs were still linked with one another, but they had faded a little, which meant, eventually, they would both be free.

Rozlyn's dress clung to her skin, the weight of it nagging at her, and the fabric itchy. Haven's shadows continued to row the boat farther south, but with no land yet in sight, she couldn't keep this dress on for the unknown length of time. She unfastened the buttons at the front of her dress and wiggled the wet fabric from her body.

"There!" She sighed in satisfaction and wrung the water from the garment before sprawling it out near her feet.

"What are you doing?" Haven hissed, snatching the fabric from the boat floor. "Put this back on. Everyone will see you."

Rozlyn took the fabric from him and rested it back where it was. "I can't very well catch a cold now, can I? And who is going to see me anyway? The dead? Besides, I don't care who looks. We all are born bare, are we not?"

Haven's lips tightened into the thinnest of lines. He then closed his eyes, chanting low words as his thumb ring changed from black to a glowing red. When he opened his lids, he knelt before the fabric and separated the dress into two. They matched in every way except one was wet and the other wasn't.

"The fabric wouldn't have dried any time soon. You can wear this one instead." He held the garment out to her, and she clasped it with a smile.

She brought the fabric to her nose and inhaled. "It smells clean too."

"You can thank my sorcery." He shrugged.

"Isn't that handy." Before she put the new dress on, she unbound her tangled hair, and squeezed the water from it. Rozlyn twisted it, then pinned her hair back around her head and slipped on the dress. "Thank you. You're kind when you choose to be." She grinned.

Haven frowned.

"It doesn't hurt to say you're welcome, does it? We're friends after all." Rozlyn winked and lifted her satchel beside her. She dug through its contents until she found a square piece of cloth, royal purple in color, and a needle and thread. Unraveling the thread, she snipped a good length off, then slipped it through the needle. As she pierced the fabric, she felt Haven's eyes on her. "Yes?"

Haven didn't utter a word as he watched her stitch a heart-shaped petal of what would eventually be a flower, when he finally asked, "What do you do with those squares? Is there even a purpose to them?"

"I usually make a quilt when I have enough of them." She smiled, recalling the one she'd last made for Cordelia. Her friend had lit up like starlight when she'd received the blue and white quilt decorated in her favorite desserts. When Haven didn't respond, she drawled, "Would you like me to make *you* a quilt? I can fashion it in all *black* squares if you wish."

He studied her for a long moment, then grunted, "I can make my own blankets."

She nudged her shoulder into his. "Is it with the same care?"

"A blanket is a blanket."

"You wound me so." Rozlyn laughed. "But you don't have to ask, I'll make you a black one when we return to the tower."

His silence meant that he most certainly would want one. It was obvious the Marquis of Shadows didn't like asking for things and found it difficult to accept gifts. Rozlyn would size his bed and make the quilt out of different black materials and textures. Perhaps stitch in parts to make it look as though shadows were in some of the squares. He would then see that a blanket was most certainly not just a blanket.

After his shadows had rescued her from the spirits in the lake, Haven had mentioned he'd only saved her because his life was dependent on hers. Even if it were true, if a spirit had taken him, regardless of the curse or coin, she would've found a way to save him. Death was nothing to him, and that wasn't something for her to judge. Only for the gods.

As Rozlyn wove the needle in and out of the fabric, Haven remained close beside her, his arm so very near to brushing hers. Her heart fluttered as he bumped into her when he hunched forward—she needed to remind herself that she couldn't develop further feelings for him. He was her patron, had her under a curse, and was in love with another. But she couldn't stop from thinking how his arm had still been around her that morning when she'd fallen asleep against his firm chest.

The quiet between them was comforting, and she wondered what he was thinking as he continued to study the floor of the boat. She tugged on the back of his hair. "You can look at the sky, you know? Take in your surroundings. No need to stay trapped in gloom all the time."

"I like gloom," he muttered. Yet he still listened to her advice and peered up at the clearing sky where at least two clouds made an appearance.

As she started to stitch her fourth flower, landscape finally approached, not a single dead tree in sight, only rows of boulders. The shadows rowed faster, cutting diligently through the water, until they reached the dock. Haven grasped Rozlyn by the waist and set her on the decaying wood before he hopped up behind her.

"Are you not going to tie off the boat?" she asked when he started walking down the dock.

"Fuck the boat," Haven said over his shoulder. "I won't need it to travel back."

"The other sorcerer was nice enough to let us use it. It's the least we can do," Rozlyn pointed out and knelt to tie the rope around the pole.

Haven's shadow slid over her, and when she looked up at him, he arched a brow, impatience rolling off of him. So she went slower as she knotted the rope to toy with him.

"You're doing that on purpose."

"*Maybe…* There!" She stood with a smile and wiped her palms against the skirt of her dress.

The dock led to an abundance of cracked dirt when they reached the end. Lines like veins spread throughout the entire area. The boulders were mostly broken or appeared as if they would collapse into fragments at any moment.

Once they skirted past the boulders, they trekked down a hill to a massive black swamp where shadows sifted through the air, weaving with one another. Not one belonged to Haven.

"What are they?" Rozlyn whispered, not wanting to draw unnecessary attention to themselves even though they could clearly be seen if the silhouettes had eyes.

"Shadows of the dead," Haven said. "While spirits can move on to the gods, the shadows dwell here. Yours and mine will both reside here one day as well. I shouldn't have to say this, but don't get near them. They are bitter creatures without their human bodies and with their spirits gone." He waved her away from the swamp. "Now, come on. We're traveling through the caverns for another day—at least then the castle is only a short distance from there."

Soon Haven would reunite with Vivienne…

Rozlyn nodded and stayed beside him as they ventured down another hill where a wide stone mouth of a cavern awaited them. She'd never once been inside a cavern or a cave before, so this was a thrilling new adventure for her.

As they drew closer to the cavern, the mouth held sharp stones, and while crossing, she wouldn't have been surprised if it closed. But it didn't.

A pleasant spicy aroma surrounded her, and they descended a set of curving stone stairs, the light behind them growing less and less until pitch-black was all she could see. But then a violet flame came to life in the center of Haven's palm. He tossed it up and the flame turned into an orb that hovered above them as they walked.

Stalactites hung all around them like icicles. In between them, a knobby texture that looked like pearls glistened beneath the glowing light. A trickle of water softly dripped into a small puddle that had collected beneath it. The path led them deeper into the earth, the stone walls holding shapes that mirrored bones.

Rozlyn trailed a finger across one resembling the lower half of a skull when movement caught her attention out of the corner of her eye. She snapped her gaze to the wall beside her, yet nothing was there except stone.

Clutching her dagger, Rozlyn found Haven further ahead, continuing at a brisk pace. As she grasped her skirts with her free hand to scurry after him, movement came once more. This time, a shadow slinked in front of her, and she thought it was Haven's, but when its freezing hand wrapped around her mouth, it was nothing like the marquis'. She tried to scream when the hand stuck to her mouth like a strip of cloth, but her voice was completely muted. When she stepped forward to run after Haven, two more wispy hands circled her ankles and yanked her not against the stone ground yet through it.

Rozlyn didn't fall to the next level but was carried by the shadows as though she were floating on air. They brought her to the stone ground, her words still silenced as she shouted. She tugged on the shadow strip binding her mouth, but it wouldn't budge. Where was she?

As she frantically spun around the room, searching for an escape, she noticed each wall held a massive hearth where blue fire crackled. A long stone dining table with eight chairs was the only other thing in the room.

No doors. Not a nook or cranny that she could wiggle through.

She peered up at the ceiling, and a mirror, instead of stone, reflected her image at her, then rippled like liquid. Atop her head rested a crown made entirely of shadows.

Rozlyn's heart thundered as four shadows danced in a circle around her, performing one perfect pirouette after another. If this had been outside a trapped room, any other time she might've clasped her hands and enjoyed the performance with a joyful smile. But not now.

Haven! she screamed inside her head as she darted

through a gap amid the dancers and dug her foot into the wall. Before she could leap upward, she slipped to the ground. It was her one escape, and one she would never reach since the walls were smooth like glass.

One of the shadows pirouetted its way toward her, halting, raising its lithe finger. Rozlyn sliced through it with her blade.

Nothing.

She was helpless, useless—something she'd never truly felt, even when trapped in Haven's tower. But she'd never been afraid of the marquis.

The shadow lifted its elegant hand higher and pointed toward the table. Rozlyn followed its finger, and this time, the table wasn't empty. A banquet of shadowed food and goblets sprawled across the stone.

Rozlyn batted a hand in the air politely. If she was to be useless in this situation, then she needed to be gracious until she could find a way to escape.

When the shadow gestured again toward the table, another presence stood beside a chair. A tall and broad-shouldered shadow that wore a crown matching Rozlyn's.

She stepped back, which only ignited a possible emotion in the shadow, and it prowled toward her. The shadow reached for her, and she dodged away from it, but when she spun to face the silhouette, it had vanished.

Something isn't right here. Her breath grew ragged, her heart elevated, as she searched the room, the dancing shadows now still as statues. Two arms clamped around her waist, and Rozlyn kicked and wriggled when the crowned shadow dragged her to one of the stone chairs. The four dancers resumed their movements, pirouetting toward her while the crowned shadow held Rozlyn in place.

The shadow's hands lifted from Rozlyn, and the gag on her mouth fell away. As she jerked forward, it wasn't her who had done the motion but her shadow, peeling itself from her body. She remained frozen, unable to rise from the chair. Her vision blurred, and the last thing she could see was the crowned silhouette draping its arm around her shadow's curvy waist.

HAVEN

Traveling through the caverns wasn't something Haven had thought twice about before, not when he generally flew wherever he pleased. After he was first summoned as a boy to this court, he'd been sent a map of the entire land and decided the only desirable way to the castle was by air. During his two-year imprisonment, he'd pulled out the old map and memorized every aspect of the court, the most obscure ways to reach Adham without being seen.

The bone-like structures surrounding Haven were about as mundane as they could come. But to Rozlyn, her doe eyes had lit up at each stalagmite, as they had with other parts of Souldark.

"It's as if you've never seen something phallic

before," Haven said as he halted his steps so Rozlyn could catch up with him.

No response.

With a frown, Haven turned around. The glow of the violet orb only reaching so far into the darkness, but she was … gone.

Had she gotten distracted? He sighed, knowing he should've carried her over his shoulder until it was time to rest.

"Rozlyn!" Haven shouted, his voice echoing throughout the caverns.

No answer. Not a sound.

"Rozlyn?" he called again, his voice gentler this time. She couldn't be far or the bonding cuff would've squeezed his wrist. The cuff had faded a little more since that morning, but that shouldn't mean the connection was severed yet.

Haven's heart lodged in his throat—if it *had*, it would take much longer to find her if she'd strayed too far. It could also mean that he would wind up back inside the tower, encased in marble, unable to drag her back to him again.

Nostrils flaring, he focused on the cuff, their link, and after only a moment, he felt her pulse. A soft, slow hum, a murmur that was unnatural compared to the other times. But Rozlyn was still *there*. Only … she wasn't in these passageways. It seemed to be coming from *below* him. *Fuck.* Had another sorcerer been hiding in the shadows somewhere? No, Haven would've noticed.

He knelt on the ground, releasing his shadows in tumultuous waves. They skimmed across the stone near his boot, and one aimed to pierce through the ground. It slammed against it and curled upward, unable to breach the surface. A *spell.* His shadows crawled up the walls to slip past the barrier, but the spell prevented them from entering there too.

As he trailed a finger over the stone, he was certain that the spell had been cast by a shadow. Who did this fucker think they were? Haven was the Marquis of Shadows, and he would annihilate anyone who took what belonged to him.

Haven slammed his palm against the stone, and his shadows mirrored his movements. His thumb ring lit up, changing from black to a deep red, the blood in his veins pulsing with rage. He growled an incantation, his words booming off the cavern walls until the stone floor disappeared, revealing a rippling silver liquid. A fucking hidden mirror. *Pitiful bastard.*

Jaw clenched, Haven peered down. Four shadows danced in the middle of a room with blue flames, circling a silhouette couple wearing wispy crowns, all spinning round and round like fools. But from the portions he could see, Rozlyn was nowhere in sight. He knew she was there ... *somewhere.* His cuff and sorcery wouldn't lie. The shadows must've hidden her.

They're all going to fucking die.

Haven grasped the edge of the slick stone, then dropped through the liquid before letting go. He landed, kneeling, and his shadows swirled around him, their wrath matching his, keeping him protected.

The dancing shadows ceased their movements, their heads slowly turning in his direction as though *he* shouldn't have disturbed *them*. His shadows whispered to Haven, and he could feel through them that the silhouette previously linked to a sorcerer was the one wearing a crown. When he was alive, he was weak—levels beneath Haven.

"Where is my wife?" he spat, his shadows weaving faster, their fury growing. One of his silhouettes tugged on his shoulder to glance behind him.

With his shadows keeping their gazes trained on his enemies, he looked behind him. Facing away from Haven, Rozlyn sat in a stone chair before a table filled with shadowed food, silhouette maggots and worms crawling over it all.

Haven rushed toward her, but she didn't move. His chest tightened when his gaze landed on her face.

Rozlyn was frozen. A human statue. Her eyes were too wide, her beautiful lips twisted in fear. Her pulse thrummed weakly through his cuff, becoming fainter with each passing moment.

The blue flames in the hearth crackled, and his eyes snapped to the other shadows who'd placed her in this decrepit state. One of the crowned figures had carried on dancing, twirling in circles around the sorcerer shadow. By the curve of her body, it was female, and she dropped to her knees before the sorcerer who pretended to be a king.

Haven's chest tightened as his gaze lingered on the shadow's bound hair around her head, the shape of her breasts, her height. *Everything.*

Rozlyn.

And her ensnared shadow was about to suck the shadow's cock.

"Stop. Now!" Haven seethed. Teeth clenched so hard they would surely crack, a raging fire churning within him, he stormed toward Rozlyn's silhouette.

His shadows shook with fury—she would suck no one's cock but his. Two of his shadows shot forward and hauled Rozlyn's silhouette from her knees. Another formed a blade and sliced through the four dancers' waists, their split bodies falling silently to the stone. Smoke rose from their wispy forms before they faded and disappeared.

The sorcerer shadow hurled pathetic inky blades at Haven that were easily knocked aside.

"Make him suffer," Haven growled. His silhouettes obeyed, rooting the shadow in place while pulling off piece by piece of the sorcerer. He wished he could hear the bastard's screams as he collapsed to his knees. With each part of him thrown to the ground, smoke seeped up until there was nothing left.

Satisfaction filled him at the sight, and he whirled around to find Rozlyn's shadow still hovering outside her body. She writhed in one of his silhouette's grip, fighting him while trying to dance instead.

Haven's boots stomped against the cavern floor as he approached the shadow, and she stilled, peering up at him.

"You will return to your body. Now," he demanded.

She resumed wriggling, her legs kicking in some sort of foolish dance. He lifted his hand where another of his shadows waited in his palm. "Get her back in her body."

In answer, his shadow lengthened, taking the form of Haven's build. The silhouette sauntered to Rozlyn's shadow and lifted her chin with his forefinger. He trailed his other digits down her side and circled his arm around her waist, pulling her flush against him.

Her dancing slowed until she became captivated by his silhouette.

His shadow held her close, spinning her around and around in a slow, seductive dance until they neared the table. The shadow leaned close to her ear, whispering something Haven couldn't hear. Her head fell back in what he could only assume was a giggle by the way her shoulders shook. Haven stayed focused, impatient for Rozlyn's shadow to return to where she belonged.

His shadow lowered Rozlyn's silhouette into her body without a fight, her wispy form disappearing.

With a gasp, Rozlyn jolted forward, and Haven caught

her as she stumbled forward.

"Are you all right?" he asked. When she only blinked, he lifted her chin with a forefinger as his shadow had done to her silhouette. "Rozlyn, can you hear me?"

Her light brown eyes held his, her breath and pulse steady. "You look worried, but I'm fine. I would never let you become stone again," she whispered and collapsed against his chest, her eyes falling shut.

Haven was a fucking bastard, and she never should've started to care about him. The least he could do was get her out of this room.

While lifting her into his arms, he waved a hand through the air. Cracking reverberated across the space as rectangular stones pulled from the wall and fashioned a staircase leading toward the mirror in the ceiling.

Haven held Rozlyn's warm body close as he carried her sleeping form up the stone steps, his shadows watching from every angle for anything insidious.

Once he passed through the rippling liquid, he cast a spell, the mirror vanishing and replaced with stone.

As he carried Rozlyn a little further, she stirred against his chest. "Haven," she whispered. "I'm sorry. I think I triggered the shadows when I touched the stalagmite."

"I should've been watching you more closely." Haven had made a mistake by not having her close to him, but that wouldn't happen again.

"All I remember was that my shadow was taken." She sighed, her voice no longer exhausted. "And then you catching me before I fell."

"It doesn't matter. Your shadow was under a spell, but I got there in time before anything other than dancing occurred." Slicing the shadows into two wasn't fucking enough. He should've picked the dancers apart piece by piece the way he had the sorcerer.

He righted Rozlyn on her feet and caught the way she watched him—as though he were her hero. That was the furthest thing from the truth. "You won't become stone," he said.

"What do you mean?" She wrinkled her nose.

"If something happens to me, you won't turn into a gargoyle outside my tower. I lied about that." He waited for her to grow angry with him, to shove at his chest, to curse him.

"Ah." Rozlyn smiled.

Why was she fucking smiling instead of raging at him or trying to escape. "Aren't you going to call me a bastard?" He would've done much more than that if the situation were reversed.

"No," she said. "Telling me the truth means you're letting someone in. Friends, remember?"

Haven scowled at her words, at how good she was. He couldn't look at her anymore or he would start to dig deeper into himself. "Stick close, or I'll have to chain our wrists together."

Haven and Rozlyn wandered down a narrow tunnel, the rough walls pushing into his broad shoulders, and the ceiling brushing his scalp. They shimmied through a thinner section, and he grunted when stone dug into his abdomen.

As they stepped into the next chamber, the air muggy, he paused—lavender and vanilla tinged the spicy scent.

Haven recognized the spell instantly. It would fuck with anyone who entered, draw their fears out in the most efficient way. A dusty yellow sky hovered above them, even though he knew it was nothing but limestone. The walls were stucco, the ground packed dirt instead of stone. Birds cawed in the distance, mournful and long. Potoo birds. *Poor me*, they seemed to cry.

Poor fucking me.

"None of this is real," he told Rozlyn. "Don't touch anything unless you want your fears to overtake you."

"I certainly won't," she promised.

Thick walls loomed on either side of them and another directly in front of them, reminding him of the labyrinth in his tower. If anyone could get past the entrance of his labyrinth, it changed to suit those who entered. He'd created the place to instill true fear in his enemies, to torment them until their hearts gave out. And before their death, they would regret *everything*.

But this was pathetic compared to his creation.

Two paths appeared before them—right and left. Each curved so it was impossible to see more than a few steps in.

Haven released his shadows to see which route they

should take. The path to the right would drain the victim in seconds, turning them into a husk. The left was nothing but an endless loop.

Closing his eyes, he pressed two fingers to his thumb ring and repeated an old incantation. The spell on the right shoved into his, but he slammed it back, choking it until the sorcery faded, leaving only a simple cavern before them.

He clasped Rozlyn's hand and held it tightly. "Don't let go of me until I say."

ROZLYN

Rozlyn kept a steady grip on Haven's hand as they traveled the winding caverns. This time they came to a stop in front of three pathways, and he released his shadows while she glanced down at her cuff, noticing that it had grown more transparent, its surface softer. Soon, the curse would wholly fade.

It was a relief that she wouldn't be cursed to stone if something happened to Haven. And, while, yes, some, including Madam, would've said to take the dagger to the deceiver's heart for lying, she wouldn't. At least, not to him. The Marquis of Shadows didn't have to reveal the truth, but he had.

The shadows drew back and motioned toward the left

chamber, so Haven led Rozlyn down the path. If it hadn't been for the bonding cuff, she wasn't certain if Haven would've found her in the shadows' secret lair. If she'd remained in a frozen state, her heart could've halted and her silhouette might've become a prisoner forever. But she also believed that her shadow would've eventually broken free of her enchantment, killed them all, then slipped back inside Rozlyn's body.

Rozlyn thought again about Madam and wondered how much the caring woman missed her. Which courtesan had Oscar ended up choosing for his journey, and had they already returned? Had Lucius gone to Cordelia since Rozlyn hadn't been there? Who was mending the other courtesans' dresses in her stead? She hadn't imagined she would be gone so long and doubted anyone else did either.

Chewing her lip, she couldn't fight the urge to peer at her cuff once more. How long after they visited the castle would the marble vanish from her and Haven's wrists? And if Vivienne did sense she'd made a grave mistake by choosing the lord over Haven, then reunited with the Marquis of Shadows, how would that make Rozlyn feel? Especially if the cuff remained for a while longer, and she had to linger at the tower, snipping off locks of hair and giving them to Haven after him and his perfect match had just pleasured one another the night before. Would her heart continue to flutter when she looked into his pale eyes, or would she be resigned and happy for her friend?

Taking a deep swallow, Rozlyn cleared her thoughts. *I would continue as I always have, distracting myself with fabrics, until it was time to leave the tower. I would then hold onto the good moments with the marquis and focus on making others and myself happy through dresses at the new shop that I'll finally purchase. But—*

Stone rubbing against stone echoed through the cavern, cutting her thoughts. Haven drew Rozlyn close to his side, and she craned her neck, peering around through the violet light of his orb. No shadows other than Haven's slinked about.

"Something isn't right here," he said, his voice holding an edge.

The grating sound erupted again, and large fragments of stone rained from the ceiling. Haven and Rozlyn dodged a sharp piece that could've easily sliced them into two. As they darted out of the way of a massive, rounded rock, the stone beneath Rozlyn and Haven's feet vanished, and she caught the edge of the ground with her free hand, his grip still in hers, preventing their fall. He didn't feel as weighted as he should've, and she noticed he'd already released his wings, lightly swishing them in the small space. If he'd tumbled down, he would've landed on shards of glass that covered the dirt below like spears.

"Stay as close to the stone as you can," he shouted.

Rozlyn used both hands to grasp the edge, the muscles of her arms growing weaker with each moment that ticked by.

Haven opened his wings as far as he could in the space, but it was enough to jolt him upward, squeezing past Rozlyn without one of the appendages slicing her. If his wing got caught, and he plummeted to the ground, he would've been no more.

Grasping her by the arms, Haven pulled Rozlyn out as her fingers slipped further. His arms held her against him while stepping backward just when the ground gave way, the stones crashing against the glass spears, the sound reverberating throughout the caverns.

A spear to the stomach was not the way Rozlyn wanted her day to end. She sighed in relief and peered up at Haven. "Just a little pitfall on our journey is all."

"Something's fucked here," he said, his scowl deepening. His fingers trailed a wall, his ring turning seafoam green. "There's old sorcery…. Very old. Keep your eyes open. The caverns should've been easier to go through than the shadowland."

"As my friend Cordelia would say, this is sheer folly, *but* I have faith in your sorcery."

"I said it's old, not that it's better than mine," he drawled. "This has *nothing* on my ability."

"I believe you." Rozlyn nodded.

They continued through the tunnels, weaving around stone wall after stone wall, all the while she kept her eyes peeled for any magical trickery. Mostly the ground, since spells had affected stone beneath her feet on two occasions now.

After a long while of walking, thighs aching, Rozlyn tugged Haven's arm to stop for a moment. Her thirst remained sated, but she needed to catch her breath. Haven looked as though he wanted to argue, yet he stood beside her and took out his flask and drank from it as her chest heaved.

She kept her gaze trained on the ground when a sharp pain clamped down on her right shoulder. "Ow," she yelped, clasping the spot and whirling on Haven. "Did you just bite me with your shadows again?"

Haven yanked Rozlyn to his chest and moved them away from the wall. "My shadow didn't *bite* you last night. It was just a small nip."

"Well, *something* just bit me," she said as she surveyed the wall behind her but found nothing except a few hairline cracks running up the stone's length.

"Stay away from the wall while I do this." Haven held up his hand, chanting words she couldn't decipher, his shadows seeping out of him, rising and curving so it looked as if they were the top portion of a throne.

And then, inside the stone, an oval shape appeared. But not just any shape, a face that protruded from the wall. One without eyes. Only a nose and sharp teeth that snapped at Haven.

"Fuck you," Haven growled and rotated his hand before slashing across the air. A crack ran across the wall, the sound as silent as the face had been when it extended its head out of the stone to bite Rozlyn. The face's mouth opened in terror, a scream that didn't make any ruckus, and then the ghastly thing was gone.

Rozlyn patted the marquis' shoulder. "Well done."

He arched a brow at her, and when his gaze trained on her lips, she could've sworn his pupils were dilated. Yet then he grasped her hand and tugged her along with him. She walked carefully beside him, watching their steps, feeling for any loose stones beneath her feet as she studied the walls for any sign of something out of the ordinary. However, the stalagmites in the open cavern they entered looked as if all of them could hold sorcery, but Haven shook his head. As he was about to step into a hole that resembled stone, she drew him aside.

Yet, thankfully, no sorcery there either.

Up ahead, at the end of the large cavern room, a fork caught her attention. Rozlyn ticked her finger back and forth between them, debating which path Haven's shadows would say was the right one to follow.

"I'll guess right," she cooed.

Haven closed his eyes, his inky darkness weaving down both tunnels. "Left," Haven said, tucking her close to his side as they entered the narrow passageway, making her lungs tight when she breathed.

They turned left and hit a dead end—a pockmarked wall stood from floor to ceiling before them.

"Should we have gone through the other passageway?" Rozlyn asked. His shadows hadn't been wrong before, but there was always a chance one could've made a mistake.

Furrowing his brow, he pressed his palm against the stone. "No, it continues through this wall."

A wall shot up from the ground mere inches from brushing the backs of Rozlyn's boots. She squeaked and bumped into Haven as she jolted forward. Spinning around, she studied the new wall that left them no space to go backward. All four walls closed them inside the space that was only a little larger than the closet they'd slept in the prior night.

A pit formed in Rozlyn's stomach while Haven pushed against the wall that would lead to the continued pathway, then slapped it. "Trickery and sorcery. *Pathetic.*"

Rozlyn tsked. "Perhaps it was one of the lords who did this to prevent anyone from sneaking to the castle."

"If it was Adham, he paid someone. His spells are average at best. And—"

The walls vibrated, and the ground shook, interrupting Haven. The tiniest of holes appeared in the walls—Rozlyn yanked him back toward the center of the space, wrapping her arms around him just as the holes became larger and spikes pierced through the walls, circling them in every direction. The only safe spot was the stone below their feet.

"Give me a moment," Haven said, his nostrils flaring. Rozlyn's arms dropped from around him, and the walls quaked again. The spikes lining the wall extended even further to where they were a finger-size away from sliding into them. How much longer did Haven have to get rid of them?

He squared his shoulders, the muscles in his chest taut, the veins in his neck bulging. Holding both hands up, he turned his arms until his palms faced the ceiling. A violet light poured out from him, cloaking the spikes. The color became translucent, then changed the spikes to a grayish hue. Cracks broke out across them, their metal surfaces morphing into grains before falling to dust on the ground.

Haven raised one of his hands higher, and his other fell to his side. The walls shook, stone rubbing stone stirring, and Rozlyn thought a new set of spikes were returning when his sorcery and shadows lifted the wall into the ceiling.

Rozlyn blinked, her eyes widening at what rested before them. Skeleton after skeleton lay sprawled across the ground. Not a bone missing, but pristine and perhaps a little bit dusty. *And* another wall blocking their way…

"I suppose this room is worse than the nails if at least ten people died here," she said, her heart pounding against her ribcage.

"They didn't die here," Haven clarified. "They were *brought* here." As the words left his lips, creaking echoed from the remains, the skeletons rising from the floor. "Keep them away while I work," he instructed.

Even in this predicament, she smiled that he

requested her help. Her dagger would do no good against bones, but she would still fight. She stepped in front of Haven when he chanted, his words melancholic and lyrical this time.

As one of the skeletons scuttled toward them, Rozlyn lunged at it and kicked the frail thing in the chest, its bones clacking to the floor. They weren't very strong at all. She slammed her foot into another, and another, and another, but the skeletons didn't stay down—they continued to rise. While keeping this up, she knew the only way she and the marquis would fail was if Haven's spell didn't work and she grew too exhausted to fight any longer. But then the skeletons turned from alabaster to gray, and their bones scattered across the ground, bursting into ash as the spikes had.

"You did well," Haven grunted.

Rozlyn grinned, her chest heaving. "A task well done. You wouldn't happen to have a spell to stay awake, would you?" she asked while stepping through the ash.

"That spell would kill you once it wears off. First, your body would swell painfully, then your bones would rip through your flesh as your organs shrivel until your breath ceases."

She blinked rapidly. "That sounds quite *lovely*."

20

HAVEN

Once Haven lifted the next stone wall, and he and Rozlyn left the skeleton dust behind, the spicy scent of the caverns dissipated. He concentrated on the magic of his ring, his shadows, attempting to see if he could locate any more hidden sorcery. It seemed to be gone, but he could've been wrong. Fucking again.

No shadows stirred, nor did traps appear as they traveled further down a stone staircase. Haven glanced at Rozlyn, and he could see she was exhausted. It was obvious in the way her lips were parted, her eyelids drooped, her shoulders sagged. He wouldn't overwork her. She'd kept the skeletons away while he'd concentrated, and dare he admit it, he was impressed. She hadn't even complained—not even now when she looked as though she could collapse at any moment.

They approached a small nook on his left, and it was the perfect place to rest for the night.

"We should get some sleep," he suggested, grasping her arm and pulling her to a stop.

"Wonderful." She sighed with a tired smile.

While he thought they were free from danger now, there was no being too careful. "My shadows will keep watch."

"Perfect." Rozlyn sank down on one side of the nook and Haven rested across from her. He should've found somewhere with less space so she would have to nestle against him like before, but she could fully stretch her muscles in here. She deserved that.

After Rozlyn removed her satchel, she leaned over on her knees and placed a soft kiss to his cheek. "Goodnight."

Haven's breath hitched, caught off guard. "Night," he said. Rozlyn showed affection quite easily—likely from her profession—but even if she wasn't a courtesan, she seemed like the kind of person who would anyway. Haven released two of his shadows to keep watch, another as a barrier across the opening, warding the area from danger.

Then he studied Rozlyn's delicate features as if he hadn't already memorized them. She wasn't quite as beautiful as Vivienne, but she was special. There was something about her… He didn't know what to do with that thought.

The next day, after Haven collected another lock of Rozlyn's hair, they continued on in comfortable silence. They passed glistening limestone and walked uneven paths. No sorcery woke to harm them, though he kept a keen eye open in case that changed.

"Today has been rather uneventful," Rozlyn said, breaking the quiet as she adjusted a loose pin in her hair.

"Do you *want* more skeletons to rise?" Haven drawled. "Because I can make that happen, only mine wouldn't fall to pieces with a kick to the ribs."

She waggled her brows. "Iseult might be envious if you did."

"He wouldn't know what to do with himself if I brought another assistant home." Haven chuckled, then tightened his jaw, realizing his mistake. She'd made him *laugh*. A laugh he hadn't released since … he didn't even fucking know. Perhaps when he'd been younger with Vivienne, before they'd taken their match to the next level. Once she moved into his tower with him, they'd both changed. The sex had always been euphoric, but had he ever smiled when she was there? Had Vivienne?

The soft trickling of water filled the air. Blue luminescence glowed ahead, and as they drew closer, wispy smoke wafted off a large lagoon at the far side of the grotto. In the corner, a small waterfall poured against glistening limestone.

"Something wonderful at last!" Rozlyn squealed and fumbled to remove her boots.

"What are you doing?" Haven asked when she dipped her toes into the water.

"A bath would be magical. It's been *days*." Rozlyn pulled her toes out. "Unless you count the lake when I was hauled in by the dead souls. Which I do not." She drew her foot back. "Perhaps you should see if anything is lurking in the water first."

Haven knelt by the lagoon, finding himself hopeful that it was safe. He desperately needed a bath too. Sex, dirt, and grime all lingered on him. The water was warm and silky-smooth when he lowered his hand into it. He released his shadows, allowing them to glide through the water's depths, searching for anything deadly, but they found nothing.

"It's fine," he said as he stood and wiped the water droplets against his trousers. The grotto was small enough to defend if things changed but large enough that they could get comfortable. "We can rest here tonight."

"I agree. But a bath first." Rozlyn loosened the buttons of her dress and a smile spread across her lips. He couldn't tear his gaze away from her ... giddiness over something so simple as a bath. She peeled the fabric from her body, revealing her large breasts. He'd touched them, tasted them, but hadn't truly appreciated them. So even though he should've averted his gaze, it remained trained on her as the dress pooled to the ground.

He wondered if she'd ever been shy about her body. The first time she'd performed as a courtesan had she blushed, or was she already used to naked bodies parading around the brothel? He liked that she was comfortable in her own skin, wasn't bashful around him.

Haven watched the curve of her backside as Rozlyn pranced into the lagoon. She walked a few more steps, her hands caressing the top of the water, drifting through the smoke, before she dipped below the surface and came up again near the cave wall. Her fingers combed back her hair, and she turned to face him, hiding all but the swells of her breasts. He wanted to see them fully again, wanted to feel the weight of them in his palms, yearned to fuck them with his cock.

"Are you coming? It's big enough that you don't have to bathe near me." As her eyes met his, they lit up in a way that Vivienne's never had. He ran a finger along his jaw. It was clear that Rozlyn didn't think of him as just a patron.

The more he studied her, washing her creamy skin, he itched to go in, to taste her, but a new and unexpected emotion washed over him. Haven didn't want to hurt her. He might not have cared before, but as he'd spent more time with her, gotten to know her, he found that had slowly changed.

Still, his revenge plan remained. Kill Adham, become Lord of Souldark, and take Vivienne as his lady. The match had always been a necessity, their fate. But in that moment, he wanted nothing more than to lose himself in pleasure with Rozlyn.

Haven stood, his body moving on instinct as he gave himself over to temptation. He snapped his fingers and his clothing disappeared. Without removing his heated gaze from Rozlyn, her pouty mouth, he slipped into the water and crept closer to her, his length hardening. "I think I'd prefer to bathe *very* close to you." He wound her hair around his hand, then tugged it back, his other arm circling her waist. Her body pressed to his as he trailed kisses up the curve of her neck.

"I would like that very much," she breathed.

Her fingers dug into his shoulders as he backed her against the wall. One of her hands skated down his chest, her digits curling around his cock. She stroked him and he groaned while nipping at her ear. But, as good as it felt, he had other plans in mind.

"I want to taste you now." Haven grasped her wrist and pulled her hand away, his cock instantly missing the touch.

Rozlyn gasped when he lifted her above him, her legs coming down over his shoulders. He took in her beauty, the scarlet curls, then licked up her warm cunt. She was as sweet as honey, and his cock twitched, precum leaking from the tip.

She twined her fingers in his hair and gripped it as he dipped his tongue inside her heat, plunging and devouring, circling and consuming. He liked the way she writhed against his face, and even more so when he slid his shadow hands up to her breasts, their thumbs stroking her nipples. A few more skimmed up her neck, tangling their inky fingers into her hair, her back arching in pure bliss until her body trembled while she moaned. She released one last quake. "Haven," she whispered as though he were her savior.

Vivienne had never once called his name when she climaxed. There'd been times with his match where he'd only cared about getting himself off, leaving her unsatisfied. But she never wanted him to continue touching her after he came either.

He gently brought Rozlyn down into his arms, cradling her close as he carried her through the water to the ledge beside the lagoon, where the steam from the water danced.

As he pulled himself from the water and aligned his body with hers, her doe eyes stared up at him. He stilled, realizing that he didn't want to fuck her roughly this time. This time he wanted to have her in a way she deserved, a way that she probably never had from any other patron. He yearned to capture those lush lips with his, kiss them thoroughly. Not knowing what that would mean for him, he brushed his lips against her neck once more instead, his shadow gliding its fingertips between the valley of her breasts.

The tip of his cock teased her entrance before he buried himself in her. He groaned at how her walls clenched around him, and she moaned exquisitely when he thrust inside her, slow and deep. He would make certain she was taken care of, that she would feel every inch of his cock.

Haven rolled his hips and she dug her nails into his skin. Rozlyn's body trembled and her center tightened around his length as she gasped. Her fingers slipped down to his buttocks, and he picked up his pace. Their bodies slapped together with each thrust until a guttural roar escaped him.

He pulled out of her and attempted to calm his breathing. After a long moment, he rolled to his back, dragging her with him. He held her against his chest as the gentle steam from the water skimmed across their bodies.

And he didn't want to release her.

21

ROZLYN

Rozlyn cracked open her eyes, the soft blue glow of the grotto enveloping her. Wispy smoke curled above as her head rested against Haven's firm chest, and her heart sang. She'd told herself over and over again throughout the years to never fall in love with a patron. There had never been one who she'd been close to feeling that way about. Thinking a patron was handsome? Many times. But not falling for one like she was doing now. No matter that the Marquis of Shadows was seeking out his perfect match. The way the butterflies swarmed in her stomach was a secret she would keep stitched away behind a barrage of fabrics and threads. No other would ever know of the words she'd spoken inside her mind.

However, she couldn't *not* think of the night before and the way Haven had pleasured her so remarkably. As he'd buried himself inside her, he'd been gentle, slow, precise, seeming to make certain he would hit every petal of her flower just right, alighting each and every nerve until she fully bloomed. It was as if he hadn't wanted the pleasure to end as much as she'd wanted it to go on forever. If this was to be their last time resting beside one another before they reached Souldark's castle, and he declared his undying love for Vivienne, Rozlyn wanted one last experience. To please him in the way he had her when his tongue had swirled and kissed up her center. Haven's cock had been inside her mouth on the night they'd consummated, but he hadn't come on her tongue, and she yearned to taste him at least once. If she didn't, she would spend her days working at her dress shop, wondering what it would've been like all while he was settling into Souldark's castle. Even if Vivienne didn't choose Haven, the Marquis of Shadows would still end the lord's life and claim the throne as his own. That would never change.

As she peered up at Haven's sharp features, for once, the line between his dark brows was smooth. The past three sleeps when she'd taken a peek at him, the line had always remained there as if he couldn't relax, even in sleep.

Rozlyn lifted off his warm chest and crawled forward, kissing the slope of Haven's neck, flicking her tongue against his salty skin, and he groaned. "Would you like me to venture lower?" she whispered in his ear.

"Yes," he rasped, his arm anchoring around her waist, his other hand drifting down her spine and cupping her backside. Heat spread low in her stomach at his touch, but this moment was meant for him.

Rozlyn ignited flames of kisses down Haven's taut chest, his muscular abdomen, until she reached his glorious cock, already wide awake for her.

She grasped his manhood and leisurely licked up his shaft, then sank her mouth over his velvety flesh. Haven fisted her hair, and she catered to him as a courtesan would, as someone who cared about him should. It was an act she'd never minded, that she always considered a simple task, but it didn't feel that way now—she delighted in her own pleasure in hearing his uneven breath, his deep lustful sounds. His body tightened, then jerked, his cock twitching as he spilled his flavor onto her tongue. She swallowed the Marquis of Shadows' delicious saltiness down, and her gaze met his from her lowered position.

"Mmm," he said, then grasped her arms and pulled her up to him so her face hovered above his. "That's something I wouldn't mind waking to every morning." A smile curled his lips. Not a smirk but a *smile*. A dazzling one that lit up his whole face. Whether he was brooding or smiling, there was beauty in them both, but she rather liked this expression he was showing her. Akin to a secret between them.

A lock of his white hair was stuck to his cheek, and she tucked it away from his face, his blue eyes watching her every move. "I've never seen irises as pale as yours. They're beautiful."

He moistened his lower lip before speaking, his smile becoming a smirk again. "My hair was black and my eyes brown until I fucked up a spell."

Rozlyn traced a finger over his lips and drawled, "I thought you've only fumbled a spell *once*."

Haven rolled his eyes. "I didn't fumble *exactly*. I was trying to create a spell so I could shift like some of the other sorcerers in Grimm. It drained a little more energy from me than it should've. I was four and still learning, so I don't count it."

"You were that powerful at *four*?" Rozlyn's lips parted. She had started sewing at an early age, but this was different.

"Of course. I built my tower with sorcery at three." He shrugged, his amused gaze locked on hers. "I traveled to all the courts after that. Except I didn't visit Souldark until I was eleven when I'd received word from the lord requesting a spell. Souldark frightened my mother, so I'd stayed away before that."

"Do you miss your parents?" If something happened to Madam, there would be more times that she would think about her than not.

"She was a good mother, but I wouldn't say I miss her. My time with her was a series of fleeting moments in my past, like all things."

"I wouldn't say that's true," Rozlyn said. "You still think of Vivienne. When did you know you were in love with her?"

Haven's frown returned. "Vivienne is my match. She was a close friend, a confidant, a sorceress whose spells made mine stronger."

Rozlyn cocked her head. "I don't believe that answered my question."

"Love isn't always necessary."

She blinked at his unexpected words. Haven was doing all of this, setting his sights on revenge, attempting to win Vivienne back after killing Adham and claiming this court as his own, because of his *sorcery*? Not because he loved her?

At the brothel, love wasn't necessary either, but courtesans and patrons both understood that. If one happened to fall in love with the other, they knew beforehand that they weren't meant to. Occasionally, they would get married, but it was extremely rare.

"I won't tell you what your decision should be, Haven," Rozlyn said softly. "But, I will tell you this—a right choice for you might be a wrong choice for me, one that I would never make. If you don't love Vivienne, and you're destroying her happiness for revenge, then you might want to think more on the matter. Love was at least *something*, a *reason*. You're already the most powerful sorcerer in Grimm, even without her."

The edges of Haven's lips curled up, except this time, the smile was cruel. "Have *you* been in love before, Rozlyn?"

Her words caught in her throat, and she cast her gaze away from him so he couldn't uncover how she felt.

"You are now, aren't you?" he cooed. "You know better than anyone not to fall for someone who could never return your affections."

Rozlyn fought the tears building in her eyes, but they filled them anyway. As her body started to tremble, she peeled herself away from him. With every patron, through every experience, not once had anyone made her feel like this, so hollow, and from one simple sentence. However true the words he'd spoken were, the way he said them was as cruel as his expression. And he'd said them purposely to hurt her.

Rozlyn was foolish, but her kindness was a trait she couldn't help. She wouldn't listen to him berate her for emotions she couldn't control. As she reached for her dress, Haven's hand snaked around her wrist, and she yanked out of his grip.

"Rozlyn, look at me," Haven said as he edged closer.

She ignored him and picked up her garment when he placed his hand gently against her cheek. "I'm a selfish bastard," he said, his tone not delicate in the least. "You knew this."

"You don't even know how to give a simple apology!" she spat as true anger coursed through her for the first time. Here. In this cavern. With him.

"Fuck it all." He sighed. And then his lips were on hers, the dress falling from her fingers as she gasped. Rozlyn knew the Marquis of Shadows would never grovel, and she didn't need him to either. This might not be enough of an apology to anyone else, but it was to her. He'd told her no kissing on the mouth, and yet, he was kissing her as if she were his lifeline.

Haven parted her lips with his tongue, then slipped it into her mouth to caress with hers. The kiss deepened, and he lifted one of her legs around his waist, backing her into the grotto wall.

"I only meant to kiss you," he rasped, his hardened length pressing into her folds. "Not to be a selfish bastard again, but I desperately need to be inside of you."

"You are who you are, and I'm not trying to change you," Rozlyn murmured. She shifted forward so that the tip of his cock lingered at her entrance before pulling him closer. He growled as he buried himself into her fully with one deft movement.

Haven squeezed her thigh as he thrust, and she met him with her rhythmic movements, increasing the friction for them both. She dug her fingers into his back so hard that bruises would be left behind. He kissed her thoroughly while his cock continued to massage her core. These sensations were *everything*, akin to the sun bursting into beautiful golden orbs at any given moment.

When pleasure blossomed inside Rozlyn, her fingers

somehow bit into him even more, their bodies both erratic and creating perfection. And as she moaned, her orgasm rolled through her in a way that not only made her quake but nearly made her shatter into smiling and satisfied fragments on the cavern ground. Only a short moment later, Haven shouted, his thrust slower, and he pressed into her again, spilling inside her and whispering, "Rozlyn."

Before he pulled out of her, his lips came to hers once more. And this wasn't just any kiss—it was a kiss that stories could be told about, that one could only wish for, that a courtesan wasn't aware she could truly want.

As Haven's lips left hers, his gaze didn't waver. "Once we arrive at the castle, I'll announce a duel with Adham instead of murdering him outright. That's as far as I'm willing to budge. I'll win in the end anyway."

It was something she hadn't expected or asked for, but she knew he was doing it for her. Rozlyn placed a hand on his cheek. "That's fair. Maybe you're not entirely selfish after all."

Even though the way he would become the Lord of Souldark had changed, she didn't ask him what would become of Vivienne because the answer would be the same. And, for Haven's happiness, at least if he didn't murder the lord outright and won a duel instead, Vivienne might accept being his match again.

However, Rozlyn's own heart had swelled. She'd fallen, hopelessly and recklessly in love with an unattainable man, but she would find a way to persevere as she had her entire life. A courtesan must do what was necessary.

Once they dressed, they passed through a few more passageways in the cavern, but it didn't take much longer for them to come out of an opening at the bottom of an alabaster hill. The warm sun shone against her face, and she breathed in the pine air.

Rozlyn's lips parted when she absorbed her surroundings—the world wasn't truly alive here but more so than in any other part of Souldark with translucent grass and gray leaves in trees that nearly looked palpable. Sorcery at its finest. A village of chalky white cottages and black thatched roofs were sprinkled throughout rolling black hills, and in the middle of it all rested a castle made entirely of what appeared to be bones.

She blinked. "That looks *cozy*. Are they real?"

"The ones inside are."

22

HAVEN

Rozlyn's kiss would easily bring Haven to his knees, influence him to perform whatever sorcery she asked for. He hadn't known a kiss could be anything close to that. Sex had always been good with Vivienne, but their kisses had never made his blood run so hot in his veins.

Because of Rozlyn, he would offer Adham a fucking duel over outright ending his life. He'd never once considered it, and if he'd been asked weeks ago, the suggestion would've been denied. What was he doing? Defeating the lord during a duel would be no challenge, and it was still an opportunity at a fair beginning. Adham would believe triumph was a possibility. Then, once Haven won against Adham, he was certain that Vivienne would take him back as her match. The rewards would be agreed upon before the duel began, of course.

As Haven walked alongside Rozlyn through the village, he watched as she studied the court with wide eyes. The false gray grass and leaves that were grown with sorcery, and the castle that resembled bones hadn't even impressed him as a child. Yet Rozlyn was easily captivated by things—something about that made him smile.

He didn't love Vivienne—that was quite clear. But her sorcery would still be beneficial to him… As selfish as he was, after hearing how Rozlyn felt unloved by her mother before she was abandoned, he would never ask her to become like her. A mistress. Never make her feel as though she were beneath Vivienne. In every way, Rozlyn was much more precious than that.

Perhaps there could be a different outcome once the duel finished…

Haven peered down at his cuff and his chest tightened when he noticed the obsidian was barely there anymore. Soon, the bargain Haven had foolishly made with Nightshade would take effect, and Rozlyn would belong to the ferryman. *No.* He would be the Lord of Souldark by then and would have the power to renegotiate. Nightshade could fuck off—Haven wouldn't hand her over to him.

"Once we reach the castle, you're not plotting to murder all the guards, are you?" Rozlyn asked. "That might frighten the village if you're going to rule here."

"I will if they get in my way." He'd planned to kill them all since they most certainly would attempt to attack him.

"You could choke them with your shadows until they passed out," she suggested. "They would wake later, albeit angry, but at least there is a chance they wouldn't rebel once you're lord of the court."

"Hmph." Except Rozlyn was right in her assumptions. He knew she didn't want to be a royal in Dawnbreak, but she would've made a fine one regardless.

At the bottom of the castle's hill, two male guards in gray and white uniforms stood watch. Haven smirked, and he waved a hand across the air. Two of his shadows drifted from him, curving around trees, slinking across the grass, then unnoticeably crawling up the guards' bodies until it was too late. Their inky hands wrapped around the men's throats, squeezing, their faces becoming cherry red and their veins bulging.

His shadows released them, and the guards slumped to the ground. Rozlyn rushed through two rows of bushes to their sides and pressed her fingers to their necks. "They still have a pulse." She beamed up at Haven. "I believe you're taking my advice then."

"Maybe," Haven grunted. He patted his pocket where the cloth doll and his spell vial still lingered. They would work better during a duel.

As they reached the top of the hill, a guard slipped out from the shadows, and before Haven let his own silhouettes take care of the issue, Rozlyn jabbed him in the throat with her fingers clamped together like a bird beak. His eyes fluttered, his knees buckling as he collapsed to the dirt.

"What?" Rozlyn smiled when she noticed Haven staring at her. "I know techniques too. And he'll wake up within the next hour."

Haven rolled his eyes and let his shadows do their work with the remaining guards outside the castle. Three guards and a servant performing sorcery on the flower garden all fell to the ground, their chests rising and falling.

Rozlyn trailed her fingers across a translucent gray flower petal as his shadows drew open the doors. They entered the castle's sitting room, and three more shadows left him, knocking out any of the guards and servants who noticed them. Except for one. His shadows held a large male guard in the air, the tips of his boots brushing the floor.

"Where is your lord?" Haven growled.

When the stubborn guard didn't answer, his shadow squeezed tighter, and the man's face deepened from red to purple.

"One more squeeze and your neck snaps, so I suggest you tell me where he is," Haven warned.

"In his room," the guard croaked.

Haven's shadow finished its work and the guard passed out just as everyone else had.

Rozlyn blinked, her lips parting in wonder as she

studied the inside of the castle. However, his expression remained the same. Over the last two years, the paintings of spirits on the walls hadn't changed. The furniture had, however. The fabrics were no longer gray but a deep blue—Vivienne's favorite color. Skulls and bones of every sorcerer or sorceress who'd ever died in the Souldark Court remained within the castle, strung across the room, running up the walls, the dome-shaped ceiling, the pillars and arches. Funerals could vary depending on the court, but when someone died in Souldark, sorcery was used to engulf the body in flames until only the skeleton remained. Their bones were then brought into the castle and hung with the others. It was considered a great honor to eternally be with the lord and lady while their soul, if not trapped here, would cross over to the gods.

"This is lovely!" Rozlyn whispered, clasping her hands in obvious elation.

He arched a brow at her. "Rooms of bones didn't strike me as your aesthetic. But since you like it so much, stay here and guard this area while I go upstairs. I'll leave two of my shadows with you to help." He paused and looked down at her. "I know you can handle this."

"Be careful," Rozlyn said. Was that melancholy reflecting in her gaze?

Haven turned away from her and ascended the wide stone staircase, the handrail coated in finger and toe bones. Two shadows trailed in front of him, and once they reached the top of the stairs, one darted down the hall to a guard standing outside the royal bedchambers. Just as the woman noticed Haven, his shadow's fingers wrapped around the guard's throat until she fell in a heap to the ornate carpet.

If Adham accepted the duel, he would be dead. If he didn't, Haven would simply revert to his first plan and kill him anyway. He'd betrayed the marquis in every sense of the word. Perhaps not as badly as Vivienne, but he'd never once attempted to speak to Haven about how he'd fallen in love with her.

Haven narrowed his eyes and stormed down the hall. He didn't pause before throwing open the chamber door, expecting to find Adham and Vivienne sweaty and tangled between the sheets despite the silence. But, when Haven's gaze settled on the bed, he stopped in his tracks. He sucked in a sharp, angry breath as he studied the still body on the mattress, her royal gray gown, her black curls. Vivienne's lips were a light shade of blue, her skin sunken and sallow. This couldn't be true. She couldn't be … *dead.*

"What are you doing here, Haven?" Vivienne gasped. Only her words hadn't come from her corpse but from the open balcony doors. A gray spirit. She wore the same clothing as her dead body, and her brow was furrowed as she peered at him. Haven looked past her to where Adham sat slumped in a wicker chair like a pauper. His button-up shirt and trousers were wrinkled, and his auburn hair hung in disarray to his shoulders. When his exhausted gaze met Haven's, his eyes were red-rimmed with dark circles beneath them, and he remained quiet, not budging from his seat.

Haven's match. The reason for everything he'd done over the last two years. Why he'd been *cursed*. Everything came rushing over him like an avalanche and all for nothing. "You murdered her," Haven growled at Adham, his shadows flooding out of him, ready to snap and tear the bastard apart. "You fucking murdered her!"

"No!" Vivienne shouted, rushing toward him. Her gray hands held up and waving in desperation, her expression panicked. "He didn't do anything, I swear it. I hadn't been feeling well for the past week, and no one knew it was my heart until it gave out yesterday. Healers tried and tried to revive me, but nothing could be done."

"*I* could've found a way," Haven seethed.

"There wasn't time, even for you. I was gone in an instant." Vivienne frowned. "Why are you here? After all this time … you've never once come to make a social call."

Haven's chest clenched at seeing Vivienne this way. Even if he'd realized she wasn't fit to be his wife, he'd never once wanted her dead. It was *Adham* who was supposed to be dead, and grieving or not, that still needed to fucking happen.

"It took me years to break a curse that would allow me to come," he admitted in a dark tone. "I didn't do all of that for a social call. You're *my* match, and even if I've grown to understand we never loved each other, your sorcery was *made* to strengthen mine."

"After all this time, you're still worried about your sorcery not being strong enough?" she scoffed. "*That* is why I left you, Haven. I was never more than *power* to you, while Adham has loved every facet of me."

Haven took a menacing step closer. "He stole something that wasn't his and it led to a very miserable two years for me."

"I apologize for making your life so miserable," Adham interrupted, his voice both dead and dripping with sarcasm. "You are, after all, the most important person in every court of Grimm. How dare we seek happiness if it meant *you* were unhappy."

Baring his teeth, Haven balled his hands into fists. "I challenge you to a duel. If I win, the Souldark Court is mine."

"You will do no such thing," Vivienne said.

"You don't have any say in the matter. He took something of mine, now I'm going to take something of his." Vivienne was meant to be included in the spoils of his win, but that had obviously changed for more than one reason. "Shouldn't you be with the gods by now?" If Adham was purposely trapping her soul here, he would kill him right now.

"I'm fighting the pull to spend a little more time with Adham. I love him, Haven. And I'm so sorry for what that meant for us. I wish I could go back and tell you how

I truly felt when we were first matched. Sometimes people are paired incorrectly, and I know deep in my heart that the matchmaker was mistaken," she sobbed.

They weren't paired incorrectly—their sorcery was a match. *They* simply weren't. Still, he couldn't listen to her anymore. Not when he had a duel to fight. Jaw tight, Haven stepped closer to the balcony doors where he faced Adham. "Do you accept the challenge? The winner gets Souldark."

"Don't!" Vivienne begged. "Just take my ring, Haven. Please. It's the source of my power and you can use it however you wish."

"I will." He cast her a sideways glance. "After I'm the new Lord of Souldark."

"Enough." Adham's dispirited gaze, pathetic and weak, met Haven's. "I accept." He sighed, not a hint of hesitation in his voice. It was obvious that, without Vivienne, the man no longer wanted to live.

"Adham!" Vivienne shouted and collapsed to her knees before him, grasping the lord's hands. "Please."

"A duel is fair," Adham said. "For getting to have you as my lady, for us loving one another, while he suffered your loss. And if I die, I'll be at your side in the end anyway. We'll do the duel now, and you, my love, will announce when we begin. Do you agree, Marquis?"

Haven's eyes narrowed. "I agree."

Vivienne didn't fight back as Adham withdrew his hands from hers and pushed up from his seat. Haven stood on one side of the room while Adham remained on the opposite end near the balcony doors. With worried eyes, Vivienne lingered in between them, across from where her dead body lay.

"When I step back from the line and say begin, then you may proceed," she said softly. "The only rule is that you may not cross where I'm standing to reach your opponent."

Haven and Adham both nodded in agreement.

Vivienne moved away from her spot and shouted, "Begin!"

Haven retrieved the doll and the vial from his trousers, the spell he'd been waiting obsessively to perform. But as he studied Adham's unmoving form, Haven didn't open the vial or chant the words. Did he forgive the lord? Fuck no. Would he give him death? Of course. But something about this was ... less than satisfying.

"At least *try*, you bastard!" Haven snarled.

Adham lifted his hand, and a blue dagger appeared. Haven grinned and hurled his shadows forward, the wispy smoke turning into a sharp blade. The lord didn't attempt to fight as the shadow sliced clean through his neck, sending his head toppling to the floor.

Vivienne screamed and knelt at Adham's side just as his gray spirit rose from the headless corpse. Haven frowned as he watched them. "You didn't need to do this!" Vivienne said, wrapping her arms around Adham.

"I never would've defeated him, my love, but I'm with you now. That's winning to me." Adham's hard stare met Haven's. "You are now the Lord of Souldark."

Somehow, it felt … hollow. Haven won, but it didn't *feel* like victory.

"Before we leave, I'm curious about one thing," Adham hedged. "A duel doesn't strike me as something you'd offer to get your revenge. You came here to murder me, didn't you?"

"Yes." Haven pulled out the doll to show them. "I planned to make birds from my sorcery pluck your eyes out while I sliced the doll's chest, effectively eviscerating you without getting my hands bloody. My shadows would've removed your heart, and I would've stomped on it in front of Vivienne, then reclaimed her. Things happened to change on the way here, and, well, I wasn't expecting her to be dead when I arrived." He shrugged.

The edges of the lord's lips curled up. "That sounds more like you."

Haven's gaze settled on Vivienne, and memories between them over the years came to mind. Their companionship. His selfishness. But her selfishness too. "You were right earlier. Our magic may have been stronger together, but you were never my match, and I was never yours."

"I've always considered you a friend, Haven," Vivienne murmured.

Haven nodded and approached her corpse. He

plucked the ring from her cold, stiff finger, and left the room, knowing the two spirits would depart the castle soon enough. Souldark belonged to him and they had no place in it any longer. And now, there was a certain woman who he needed to get back to.

As he descended the steps, he found Rozlyn gone. His frown deepened and he sprinted the rest of the way down the staircase. A relieved breath escaped him at the sight of Rozlyn near one of the chairs, her hair golden again. His shadows swirled protectively in front of her and, when he called them back, his heart sank.

Nightshade stood before her, his hands in his pockets. "Your cuff is gone," he said to her with a small grin.

Haven lifted his arm to find his cuff vanished completely, and his pulse sped, hammering through him. "No," he rasped.

Both Rozlyn and Nightshade's gazes met his, and her eyes lit up. "Haven!" But as she started toward him, Nightshade slipped his arm around her waist. He grasped her wrist to show Haven the tattoo of a crescent moon with a dark eye at its center that matched the ferryman's. "A bargain is a bargain."

Rozlyn's lips parted, confusion swirling in her stare.

"You—" Haven's words ended abruptly when Nightshade and Rozlyn both disappeared from the castle.

The court belonged to the Marquis of Shadows, but that was never what he truly wanted. It was *love* he was looking for all this time. It was *Rozlyn*, and he would get her back.

23

ROZLYN

Silver metal vines hung along the walls, flames crackled in a fireplace before an empty furred rug, and familiar furniture surrounded Rozlyn. No longer was she standing inside Souldark's castle of bones, but she was now in Nightshade's manor with the ferryman's arm still planted around her waist.

Rozlyn easily broke free of his grasp and whirled to face him. "We're at your manor," she breathed as she recalled the words he'd spoken to Haven only moments ago. *I do believe a bargain is a bargain.*

"And so we are, princess." Nightshade smirked, sauntering toward her. "Haven promised you to me once he became Lord of Souldark, so where else would we go?"

Princess. He knew her secret lineage... Had Haven truly promised her to Nightshade?

Rozlyn studied the black tattoo on her wrist that had replaced the marriage cuff to Haven. An eye in the center of a crescent moon. Was the curse between her and the Marquis of Shadows entirely lifted? She hadn't even felt the cuff vanish, had only noticed the new mark when Nightshade held up her wrist for Haven to see.

She quickly unbound her hair, yanking out pins and tossing them to the floor. When a few locks fell down her back, she drew one over her shoulder and gasped. Her hair was the color of a thousand suns again—no longer blood red.

Rozlyn would ignore the fact that Nightshade had called her princess. She wasn't certain if he'd uncovered the truth himself or if Haven had told him… Her heart clenched—he was the only one who could've given him that information. Madam never would.

"You mentioned a bargain between you and Haven. That I was given to you. What do you mean?" she asked, her heart knocking against her ribs. *Knock. Knock. Knock.* Soon, she believed they might crack if her heart raced any harder.

"Ah, that," Nightshade purred while wearing a wide grin. "So you want to get right down to the business of it all." He grasped one of the two full glasses of wine from the table and brought it to his lips, taking a slow sip. So incredibly slow as he smirked at her again. "You were just a pawn for the marquis. Everyone and everything is to him. He uses up those who will help him, then tosses aside anyone who isn't an asset to his sorcery. He came to me with quite the offer, you see, and didn't think twice when he traded you so he could reunite with his match. Someone he believes is more useful to him. But I'm not like Haven—I believe you're useful, Roz. And not to just break a curse."

His words slammed into Rozlyn like a stone to the chest. Yet one thing he said couldn't be allowed. "Traded?" Rozlyn frowned. "A courtesan of my madam's brothel can't be sold without consent."

"You weren't sold, you were traded. Besides, you're in Souldark, sweetheart. Rules are different here than in Dawnbreak. I didn't suggest the bargain, but I wasn't going to turn it down. Anyone in my position would've accepted." He shrugged and again leisurely drank from his glass while watching her, his eyes dancing with amusement. "Forget about Haven. He was always meant for Vivienne. The matchmaker told him so, and that's his fault for being foolish enough to allow someone to choose for him. Unlike me—I'm choosing *you*."

Rozlyn stepped away from him, even though she didn't believe him to be wicked. She needed to reason with him before she left his home. Bargain or not, she wasn't the one who'd made it. "I'm sorry if this hurts your feelings, Nightshade, but I'm not choosing you."

"Not yet, but you will." Nightshade sat on the settee and leaned back, then patted the cushion beside him. "Let me explain something."

There was nothing to explain that would change her mind, but she sank down next to him, so she could let him down gently once he finished. It was something she'd had to do with patrons in the past, and while sometimes they still wished for her to love them, they hadn't tried to further pursue or hurt her. But most feared Madam's wrath.

"I have a little story for you, Roz." His arm slid across the top of the settee behind her, but he didn't curve it around her shoulders. "Unlike Haven and Vivienne, you and I are truly a perfect match. Why? We're both bastard royalty. Both shunned. Both dreaming of things we can't have. Both fuck as a necessity. You for coin. Me for other reasons. And I promise I will treat you as the queen you should be. We should settle in at the Dawnbreak Palace to start fresh. Think about it."

Rozlyn's eyes widened. Settle in at the *palace*? He meant to use her so they could rule Dawnbreak? She angled her head to the side and pressed her fingertips together, pretending to mull it over. "I thought about it, and no thank you. The palace isn't my home. It's not where I want to live my life." With a pat farewell to his shoulder, she politely left Nightshade to himself and opened the door. Her breath halted in her lungs as she stared at the iron bars blocking her exit.

She gripped the cold bars and yanked on them to no avail. With what strength she had, she attempted to pry the iron apart. Nothing. No luck. It didn't even budge.

Rozlyn whirled around to find Nightshade tapping his fingers against the back of the settee while he watched her with a smirk.

"Remove these, please," she asked sweetly, her pulse racing beneath her calm demeanor.

Nightshade stood from the couch and stretched his back, then gingerly prowled toward her. "These?" He pointed toward the iron and trailed a finger across one.

"Yes."

The ferryman didn't remove or open them but walked straight through the bars. He turned to look at her with his widest grin yet. "Think about our future some more. Time is aplenty since I no longer have a duty to ferry souls to the gods. We'll have this discussion again when I return. And don't worry, Roz—what's mine is yours in the manor. Feel free to do anything you like."

"Nightshade!" Rozlyn shouted. She grabbed the bars, trying to shake them off the door. "Let me out of here!"

Without glancing back at her, he waved a farewell. Even though she couldn't see his face, she knew he was still smirking.

Rozlyn had been right about the ferryman being lonely. That was clear. But she wouldn't destroy the royal family by shoving herself and Nightshade into the palace to claim their stakes in Dawnbreak. A small amount of hope, and foolish others would say, but maybe, after everything, Haven would regret the bargain he'd made. Perhaps even come for her as he had with the shadows inside the cavern, but she had been linked to Haven at the time. He'd needed her then, yet he didn't need her any longer. Did his kiss to her mean nothing? Or was it a kiss goodbye? She knew how others would feel about him. But she couldn't bring herself to loathe him. Sometimes she wished she didn't have a heart at all, that it would be simpler than allowing hurt to wash over oneself.

Rozlyn couldn't focus on feelings now—she needed to find a way to escape Nightshade's manor. She grasped her skirts and inspected every inch of his home, throwing open door after door, discovering all the windows to be barred too. Rozlyn kicked at each one, yet it did no good. Nightshade might not be a sorcerer, but he certainly had tricks up his sleeve.

She fled up the staircase to the second floor to find the window in each room mirrored the others. The last room she checked was Nightshade's bedroom, and when she did, a whirlwind of images from the night with Haven poured over her. Nightshade's sheets had been replaced, but she could still smell a faint hint of Haven's citrus.

Rozlyn rested her forehead against the window bars. The Marquis of Shadows' tower had been a prison too, yet this was much different. The cuff linked to Haven had been temporary, something she'd known since the beginning. But this tattoo? It would be forever. Could weaken an entire court, destroy the royal family.

As time passed, Rozlyn pounded the walls to see if she could break through them, yet they were as hard as steel. She couldn't wiggle through the small chimney in the fireplace either. If anything, she wagered there were bars at the top anyhow.

No matter when or where Rozlyn was, she always found solace in stitching a fabric square, except for this one instance. Instead, she hovered by the door, for *hours*, until footsteps echoed outside it. As Nightshade stepped over the threshold, Rozlyn stuck out her foot and watched him trip to the floor with a loud curse. She flipped him to his back before pressing her dagger to his throat in the same way she had with Haven, only this time she would make him bleed.

Fear didn't stir in his gaze as a grin spread his cheeks. "So, riling you up a little is all it takes to get you in this position?"

"My blade will carve a smile across your throat if you don't make the bars disappear," Rozlyn snapped.

"Slit my throat, stab me in the heart, do what you wish because I can't die. I'm immortal," he purred. "If we marry and consummate, I'll make you immortal too. *Think* about it."

Rozlyn sliced the blade across his throat. Even though his flesh split open and blood oozed out, his bemused expression didn't change. His skin closed in mere moments, proving that he was truly the son of a god.

"That wasn't very nice." Nightshade chuckled and lifted her off him. He left back through the bars, ticking his finger at her. "I believe you need more time to think."

"Nightshade!" she shouted through the bars. "This is another curse. I won't change my mind!"

Rozlyn waited, and waited, and *waited* for Nightshade to return for two days. She'd slept, then ate and drank from his magical kitchen. The little hope she'd held that Haven would change his mind had vanished. She should've known as soon as Nightshade told her there was a bargain. Still, she'd hoped. Even if Haven didn't love her, she believed he thought of her as a friend. But friends didn't bargain with each other's freedom.

Her madam had been right. Loving a patron would not end well.

Her heart felt as if it might need stitching, but she couldn't reach inside to mend it. Tears gathered in her lashes, and she held back a sob. But when her chest tightened further, she cried, cried as she had after her mother had left her like unwanted soggy porridge.

The door opened, and Rozlyn jerked up, taking her hands from her face. Nightshade slipped inside as if he hadn't just left her ensnared in his home. The smile fell from his face when he glanced in her direction. "You're crying."

"I can't stay here," she sobbed. "I want to go home. I want to see my family. I want to make my friends dresses again."

"Fuck me, Rozlyn," he said gently, stepping closer to her. "I'll give you all those things and more when we go to Dawnbreak. You can visit your family, make as many dresses as you want. I'll pleasure you in ways that will make you forget the Marquis of Shadows ever existed."

Rozlyn peered at the floor and whispered, "I'll never love you."

Nightshade lifted her chin, his obsidian eyes promising her his words. "And I'll never love you. But, you and I, we're one and the same."

24

HAVEN

Without traveling through the caverns, the journey home would be faster. Haven flew across the dismal court for two days straight, only taking a few hours rest to keep up his strength. Even when a storm rained down its fury, he continued. *Fuck the rain.*

It wouldn't be much longer before he reached his destination. His muscles were on fire and his wings on the brink of collapse. But he couldn't stop now, not when he was so close. Two days were short compared to a lifetime, but two days alone with Nightshade might be enough for Haven to lose Rozlyn forever.

The bastard's manor finally slipped into view, complete with new additions—bars on the fucking windows and door. While remaining in the air, he reached out with his shadows, testing them. They were made with a spell using Nightshade's immortal blood. Haven was powerful, more so with Vivienne's ring, but even his shadows couldn't do anything without a concoction he had inside his tower. If that prick had touched Rozlyn in any way, Haven would break him apart, piece by piece. It might not kill the immortal, but it would hurt like a fucker. Haven fought the urge to soar to the manor now, to tell Rozlyn he would come back for her, but he didn't want to alert Nightshade. Of course, there was a chance that the ferryman might've already taken Rozlyn to another court since he was now free, but something about the bars told him otherwise.

Haven ignored the remainder of his surroundings, his gaze trained in the direction of his home. He cracked his wings harder, and his strength waned as hunger returned. *Almost there.*

The marquis' obsidian tower pulled at him like a dark beacon, and he made his descent to the entrance door. A few spirits hovered nearby in the rolling mist, but none dared to approach him. Without stopping to catch his breath, he released a shadow to unlock the door.

"Iseult!" he roared as he stormed down the cellar steps toward the spell room.

As Haven hit the last step, Iseult rushed out into the hallway toward him, a ladle in his skeletal grasp. "What's wrong, Marquis?" he asked, the shadows swirling in his sockets with worry.

"I need your help," Haven demanded, his chest heaving.

"Anything," Iseult said, bowing his head.

"Rozlyn is with Nightshade," Haven ground out as he bounded into the spell room with his assistant close on his heels. He grabbed another vial of the spells to ward off hunger and thirst. There wasn't time for him to sit down and fucking eat right now—he could feast later when Rozlyn was with him again. Then he fumbled over rows of ingredients, plucking up what he needed.

Haven snapped his fingers at Iseult. "An empty vial, quickly."

One appeared in his hand almost instantly. He shoved books out of the way and began pouring the different liquids into the empty glass while chanting an incantation. A few moments later, he corked the new spell that would counteract the bars on Nightshade's home and shoved it into his pocket.

"I was a bastard and a fool," Haven told his assistant. "I bargained Rozlyn so I could gain a court I never wanted. For a woman who I never truly loved and who never loved me. My match was right in front of me, in this very tower, bound to me for these past few weeks. There's only one thing that Nightshade won't refuse in exchange for freeing Rozlyn. You'll have to agree to it." This was the deepest Haven had ever gotten when conversing with Iseult, and even though his assistant would agree to any request, he wanted him to understand.

"Of course I will, Marquis."

If Nightshade didn't agree, Haven would spend a lifetime searching for a way to rip his immortality away. Only then could he murder the ferryman so the mark he left on Rozlyn's wrist would vanish.

Iseult followed Haven out into the mist, the air sticky. He grasped his assistant under the arms and lifted him into the air with one crack of his wings. Iseult's bones weighed practically nothing as he carried him over the gloomy landscape. Even in flight, his assistant kept his spine straight, and with Haven by his side, Iseult's bones wouldn't break apart as they would've if he were wandering the court alone.

Nightshade's manor would be approaching soon, but time seemed to drag before Haven finally touched down in front of the manor. Tucking his gargoyle away, he released Iseult, and his temper flared at the cage Nightshade had created for Rozlyn. Haven had done the same to her with his shadows, but he vowed to himself that she would never be caged again. Blood boiled in Haven's veins—he would start by ripping off Nightshade's eyelids and work his way down.

Haven's shadows shook in rage as they flew from him and gripped the bars even though it would do no good. He retrieved the vial from his pocket and poured it along the ground while chanting an incantation. The words were old, passed down from the gods themselves to one of the first sorcerers. It had stayed within Haven's family throughout the centuries. Once the final word left his mouth, his shadows pulled the iron again, and this time, they pried apart.

"Wait here," Haven told Iseult, then he hurled the door open and barged into the manor. He didn't have to venture far to find Nightshade's fingers on Rozlyn's chin, his body too close to hers.

"Release my *wife*," Haven growled, his shadows crackling like thunder around him.

"Ah, the Marquis of Shadows has arrived." Nightshade smirked, his hand falling from Rozlyn's chin. "Your marriage bond no longer exists. You gave her to me."

"You came," Rozlyn murmured, tears filling her eyes.

Haven swallowed deeply, his anger cooling as he studied her. "I should never have bargained you. It was before I—"

"Before you came to your own senses?" Nightshade interrupted and grabbed his wine glass from the table. "Regrets happen. Apologies, but there's nothing I can do about that." One of Haven's shadows shot forward and knocked the glass away from Nightshade before he could bring the wine to his lips. "What a waste." He tsked.

Haven's eyes pierced into Nightshade like icy daggers. "As lord of this court, you will obey me," he seethed.

"If only a lord's demands were worth more than a bargain." His smirk returned and he leaned against the wall with his arms folded.

"He offered me a way home," Rozlyn whispered. "And—"

"No." Haven shook his head. "Whatever he offered to you, the answer is fucking *no*." He stormed toward Nightshade, his fists shaking while holding back his shadows. "I have another bargain to offer. One that would be more useful to you."

Nightshade arched a brow. "Go on." The immortal was always willing to listen to a proposition.

"As you know, Souldark belongs to me now. I'll give the court to you. You can have it all." It would be no loss to Haven—it was never what he truly wanted. He simply wanted Adham gone and Vivienne back. But losing Rozlyn would be like cutting out his own shadows.

"Hmm, that's an enticing offer." Nightshade trailed a finger across his lower lip, and Haven was one breath away from having his shadow tear his entire hand off. "Though I *could* have Dawnbreak eventually…" His bemused gaze drifted to Rozlyn. "If I chose Souldark, it would be mine right away, but I would need a ferryman. The line has been getting rather long without me assisting the spirits across the lake. Before you offer, the gondola won't accept anyone alive unless they carry the blood of gods."

Haven knew this already, and he'd come prepared. "One moment." He summoned Iseult from outside the manor, where his assistant obediently stood waiting. After

Iseult stepped into the manor, he came up to Haven's side. Rozlyn studied them both with wide eyes as Haven said, "My assistant will be the ferryman for Fairward Lake. He's both alive and dead, an immortal in his own right. I've come up with a permanent way to keep his bones from breaking apart without me there or him inside my tower. He'll need a single drop of immortal blood."

"That's up to Iseult to decide," Rozlyn interrupted. "No one else."

"And me," Nightshade added. "But do go on, Iseult. What's your decision?"

Haven's nostrils flared—this was *his* assistant. He'd created him! But he remained silent.

Rozlyn pressed her hand to Iseult's shoulder. "Before you answer, think for yourself. Not the marquis. Not me. Not Nightshade. No one but Iseult."

Iseult nodded and turned to face Haven. "Marquis?"

"It's up to you," Haven said, resting his palm on his assistant's other shoulder. "You've been a good and faithful servant. Now you have the chance to be the ferryman and help souls cross over to the gods. You'll have your own manor."

The shadows in Iseult's eyes swirled, his jaw parting into a smile as he said, "This is an honor. I will do my best to serve you and this court."

"You'd be serving *me,* since it would be my court if I were to accept," Nightshade added and his eyes grew hooded. "I need something more."

Of course the bastard fucking did. "What?" Haven said between gritted teeth.

With a wide grin, he shrugged. "Oh, just a vial of poison made with nightshade."

That seemed egotistical and simple, *too* simple, but Haven wouldn't question it if that was all it took to get Rozlyn back. He didn't care who Nightshade used it on. "Fine."

"The Lord of Death has a nice ring to it, doesn't it?" Nightshade chuckled.

Haven rolled his eyes before focusing on Rozlyn. "Can you get us a needle from your things?"

She nodded and dug through her satchel on the table until she fished out a shiny silver needle. Haven took it from her and faced the ferryman.

Nightshade fluttered his fingers in front of Haven's face. "Take your pick." Haven ignored him and pierced his forefinger, driving the needle in farther than necessary. Nightshade didn't so much as flinch.

Iseult stepped toward them and opened his mouth. Nightshade promptly squeezed a drop of blood inside. Haven chanted the same spell he'd spoken when he'd brought Iseult to life, only this time he added a few extra lines to the incantation, his and Vivienne's rings both burning bright red. When they faded back to black, the spell was complete.

Nightshade held up his wrist where a new symbol of a bone crown replaced the crescent moon, sealing their bargain.

Rozlyn glanced at her own wrist, free of any tattoos or cuffs. "I'm still here." She blinked.

"Until I take you home. You won't be able to cross into Souldark after that." Haven shrugged.

"Well, it's been a pleasure as always, Haven," Nightshade purred. "I'll need the poison within the next seven days delivered to my castle." Then he turned to Iseult. "Come with me. I'll take you to the gondola and show you the ropes."

Rozlyn rushed forward and wrapped her arms around Iseult. "I'm going to miss you."

He stroked his skeletal hand over Rozlyn's golden hair. "Take care of Marquis."

Nightshade guided Iseult toward the door. "I believe the first spirits you have the honor of ferrying across Fairward are Vivienne and Adham."

ROZLYN

Horror washed over Rozlyn, and she spun to face Haven. Had the lady intervened when Haven dueled the lord? "Vivienne?" she gasped, noticing a new black ring on his pinky finger. "What happened? Did you do something to her?"

"*No.*" Haven sighed, his frown trained on where Nightshade had just walked out the door with Iseult. "When I found them, Vivienne's spirit was already with Adham. She'd passed unexpectedly a day before we arrived at the castle. Adham accepted the duel I'd offered, and I won. I took her ring before I left, so I'm still a selfish bastard."

A spirit could linger for different reasons, but Rozlyn

believed Vivienne had been there to stay by the lord's side a little longer. "He wanted to die to be with her, didn't he?"

"Yes." There was no emotion on the Marquis of Shadows' face, but his eyes told her otherwise.

"And you allowed it," she murmured. "You could've decided not to offer him the duel and held him somewhere in your tower to keep them apart."

"I could've. Though, I suppose he might've found a way to kill himself eventually." Haven's throat bobbed. "Vivienne might've been my match, but only because of our sorcery. I should've realized that years ago."

Rozlyn peered down at her hands. "You lied to me," she whispered. "You promised I would be free when you'd already secretly traded me to Nightshade. You could've at least warned me."

Haven stepped toward her and slowly lifted her chin with his finger. "I never lied. It was true when I said you'd be free of me."

Her heart thundered, and she wanted to hurl him out of the manor. "You—"

One of his shadows held a finger over her lips. "I'm not sorry I cursed myself because then I wouldn't have needed *you*."

It wouldn't be considered an apology to most, but it was to her. Rozlyn folded her arms around him and held him tight, tears gathering in her lashes. "I didn't think you would come."

Haven returned the embrace, resting his chin on top of her head. "I would've come to you anywhere." They stood in silence for a long while when his next words came out tight. "If I hadn't come when I did, would you have bound yourself to Nightshade?"

Rozlyn thought about Nightshade's promises and peered up at him. "I wanted to," she whispered.

A line formed between his brows and his scowl deepened. "I see."

"Not because I love him, but because I wanted to go home," she said as she stepped away from him. "But, in the end, I wouldn't have gone through with it. There's only been one man I've ever loved." *The Marquis of Shadows.*

"I like that answer. Now come." He lifted Rozlyn in his arms and held her close. "I'm taking you home."

Rozlyn grinned and didn't utter a word as Haven carried her out into the misty afternoon. His wings pierced through his back, and a gust of wind blew her hair as he soared toward his tower.

She didn't shut her eyes on the journey this time, yet she couldn't control her trembling. Every time she peeked toward the ground, her stomach dipped and nausea churned within her, but not as much as it would've before. She caught sight of Iseult and Nightshade already inside the gondola.

The heavy mist became lighter as they approached Haven's tower. More black flowers had bloomed up the vines of his home, and Rozlyn smiled. His feet touched down on the window ledge, and he helped her inside the room before shifting out of his gargoyle form.

He snapped his fingers, and when Rozlyn looked out the window, the court grew blurry before clearing to lush green foliage. Her heart beat with glee, and she rushed out of the room, fleeing down the tower steps. The door remained locked, and she bounced on the balls of her feet until Haven caught up with her.

The edges of his lips curled up as his shadow took the shape of a key. "You were faster than me this time."

Once Haven opened the door and removed the shadow barring the space for her, Rozlyn stepped out into the warm sunshine of Dawnbreak and fell to her knees in the grass. She brushed her fingertips against their velvety blades and breathed in the fresh spring air. Birds flocked toward the tower, perching atop the roof.

As she stood, Haven leaned against the stone with his arms crossed over his chest.

"What?" She smiled.

"Just waiting for you to stop kissing grass so I can give you this." He swirled his hand in the air and a large velvet bag appeared in his grasp. "Your payment."

Rozlyn blinked. The sack looked as though it held much more than would've been owed to her. If she took the money, it would mean that everything she'd done was about receiving coin. And it wasn't. "You keep it," she finally said. "You gave up Souldark for me."

Haven pushed off the wall with his boot and inched closer to her. "Souldark is an abysmal, desolate *nothing*. You earned this, Rozlyn."

Rozlyn pressed his hand holding the bag against his chest. "No thank you." She looked down at her simple black garment. "But I do think it's about time I make myself a different colored dress. Something yellow."

Haven rolled his eyes. "Who would've guessed?" He grasped a loose lock of her hair and tucked it behind her ear. "It suits you though. Go home and see your madam. There is something I need to do, but I'll meet you tomorrow before the day's end. Tell your madam I'll cover the cost of any lost earnings for you."

Rozlyn cocked her head. "What do you have planned?"

"You ask too many questions." As she opened her mouth to speak, he cut off her words with a kiss. "Now go, you're wasting time."

"Fine," Rozlyn relented, and with a smile, she clutched her dress and took off through the forest. She glanced back to find Haven still watching her, his frown nowhere to be seen. He then shifted into his gargoyle form and took off into the sky.

Rozlyn skirted around the trees until she stepped onto the graveled trail leading toward the brothel. Even though thirst gripped her, she didn't stop even when she reached the shops. She burst through the door of the brothel, and Madam jerked up from her seat behind the desk, a long cigarette in her hand.

She put out the cigarette and ran toward Rozlyn, a welcoming smile across her face. "Are you all right?"

"Yes, yes, I'm fine," Rozlyn panted and embraced Madam in a tight hug. "I chose not to take my portion of the marquis' money though."

Madam stumbled back and cupped Rozlyn's face, studying her intently until her features softened. "You fell in love, didn't you?"

"I'm sorry, Madam."

"No one can control how they feel." She kissed her on the forehead. "Where is he?"

Rozlyn shrugged. "He said he would come here before tomorrow ends."

Madam pursed her lips, and Rozlyn knew what she was thinking. That men lie. "Let me get you a cup of tea and a bowl of soup. You look as though you're about to faint."

"Thank you." Rozlyn sank down into a cloth chair and while waiting for Madam to return, Cordelia squealed and rushed into the room. "Rozlyn! You're back!" She hunched in front of the chair, and they hugged one another. "Thank goodness you missed Cleetus. He was calling on you, but Starla took him. I hope you're not upset—Lucius requested me since you were gone. I know he's yours."

Rozlyn smiled, clasping her dearest friend's hands. "You deserve a sweet client." He would treat Cordelia well.

Madam slipped through the velvet curtains with a cup of tea and a steaming bowl of soup. "A couple of the girls just had dinner so everything is still warm."

"Thank you," Rozlyn said and lifted the tea to her lips. Once she finished her meal, Madam told her to retire for the evening.

As Rozlyn left the sitting room to gather a nightgown, she chewed on her lip with a smile while wondering what Haven would say when he returned.

Throughout the day, Rozlyn, Cordelia, and Madam cleaned the brothel. They swept and scrubbed the floors until they shined like new.

When they questioned Rozlyn further about her time spent with the marquis, she confessed the story in its entirety to them both. Even the parts that Cordelia hadn't known about Rozlyn being a bastard princess, but she trusted her as much as she did Madam to keep it a secret. Madam's face turned horrified, and Cordelia sighed adoringly at the end of the story while saying, "It's beautiful that he gave up an entire court to save you."

"*What?*" Madam snapped. "She could've been held as a prisoner forever."

Rozlyn gently enfolded her hands around Madam's shoulders. "As one begins a tale, they imagine alternate endings. But once they reach the final page, they find out how the story truly concludes. My ending was coming home."

"Without coin for your dress shop!" Madam hissed. "I kept my mouth shut yesterday, but after your story, I can no longer. You should've taken the money."

"I wouldn't have taken it either," Cordelia said. "Well, maybe *some* of it."

The door opened, and they turned toward it as a tall, stoic man draped in all black entered. *Haven.* Madam and Cordelia both straightened, their eyes wide and dreamy. Rozlyn smiled, waiting for Haven to introduce himself to watch Madam's reaction.

His gaze first settled on Rozlyn with an unreadable expression before he looked at Madam and Cordelia. "I need to speak with Rozlyn. I'm Sorcerer Marquis Haven Darrow."

"Get out!" Madam snapped. "I don't care what you can do with your sorcery. After what you did to one of my courtesans, you will never step foot in this establishment again."

Haven drew out a bag of coins from inside his cloak and held it out to Madam. "I must speak with her."

"It's fine, Madam," Rozlyn soothed, patting her shoulder.

Madam narrowed her eyes at the bag but snatched it

from his hand. "You may speak with her *here*."

Haven nodded. "Of course." It was the most gentlemanly Rozlyn had ever seen him.

Madam huffed and slipped with Cordelia behind the desk, their gazes still trained on Haven. Cordelia's dreamy and Madam's still narrowed.

Haven grasped Rozlyn's hand, his thumb stroking her wrist where her marriage cuff had once been. "I want you to come home with me. Even if I have to pay you."

"She isn't going back to your wicked tower!" Madam shouted.

"Let me take you to my room where it's quieter." She signaled to Madam that all would be well, and the woman pursed her lips, seeming to wish she'd told Haven to leave instead. But this was Rozlyn choosing what she wanted— no one else.

She grasped Haven by the hand and led him through the curtains and down the hallway toward her room. His shoulders stiffened as his gaze fastened on one of the courtesans on her knees, bringing a patron's cock into her mouth as the man groaned.

"I take it you've never been inside a brothel before," she said.

"I have now."

Rozlyn grinned and pulled Haven into her room. She guided him to her bed and stood before him. "So, why is it you want me to return to your tower? To replace Iseult?" she hedged.

Haven frowned. "Because I don't want you here, fucking other men."

Rozlyn angled her head and she smiled wider. "And you want me to pleasure you instead?"

"I want to pleasure *you*," he growled. "Every day. Every fucking night. While your dress shop is being prepared."

Rozlyn's eyes widened, her heart humming. "My *shop*?"

The corners of Haven's lips turned up. "Since you refused the coin, I bought you a shop instead. If you aren't ready for it yet, it will remain empty until you are."

Rozlyn leapt forward and knocked Haven to the mattress as she hugged him.

"I assume that means yes." His eyes lit up with amusement.

"I'm considering it." She winked. "Of course my answer is yes!"

Haven closed the gap between them, his lips coasting across hers while veering his hands to her backside and bringing her closer against him. "Fuck me," he rasped. "Fuck me so that I'm the last man you ever touch in this place."

As Rozlyn reached for the button of his trousers, she drawled, "It will cost you."

"I have plenty of coin."

"It will cost *your kisses*."

EPILOGUE

HAVEN

At Rozlyn's request, Haven vowed on his life as a sorcerer that he wouldn't visit her shop until it was finished and that absolutely no spells of any sort could hurry the work along. He might've had his shadows sneak in a few helpful errands here and there, but he was growing impatient to see her reaction.

Haven stood at his cauldron, sprinkling in a few herbs before stirring the contents. Over the past two months, he'd visited Souldark once a week with his tower when Rozlyn was working at her shop. She had asked him to deliver Iseult her handmade gifts. The skeleton was happier than Haven had ever seen him, and he admitted that he rarely stayed at the manor. Instead, he spent most nights helping lost spirits so they could find their way to the gods. Haven's old assistant had no beating heart, but if he did, it would've been bigger than anyone else's. Being that selfless was something Haven could never achieve.

Rapid footsteps echoed down the stairs. Rozlyn flung herself into the spell room, her cheeks flushed pink, and a yellow lacy dress hugged her curves. The color was growing on him.

"It's finished!" she squealed and tugged Haven's hand, his boots planted to the floor. "The shop!"

"It's about fucking time," he said, fighting a smile.

"Oh, shush." She grinned. "I know you helped. I just kept quiet about it."

Haven smirked as Rozlyn dragged him out of the tower and through the forest, the giddy smile continuing to glow and light up her face. Her freckles shone like stars beneath the blazing sun, and he desperately wanted nothing but to be bound to her once more, for Rozlyn to be his wife. They'd fucked every night, made love every day, and he hadn't chained her down. That was something he would never do to her again. With Rozlyn, he'd learned what it was like to truly *feel*. But only with her. The rest of the courts could go up in flames for all he cared.

They neared the market, and bustling customers walked up and down the streets. Fresh breads and savory meat permeated the air.

Rozlyn drew to a stop in front of her shop's door,

clasping her hands as she bounced on her feet, her doe eyes lighting up even more.

Yellow drapes cloaked the windows, concealing what rested inside.

"This is it!" she chirped and opened the door. He followed her over the threshold, and his gaze swept across the sea of dresses. Every fabric and color one could imagine. Yellows, greens, purples, blues, a rainbow of colors each in their own section of hues.

"This is … lovely," he lied.

Rozlyn placed her hands on her hips. "Thank you for pretending to like them. But! You didn't look in the back yet." She waggled her brows and grabbed his hand once more and guided him past a velvet curtain to reveal a room entirely of dark dresses. Ball gowns. Simple dresses. Ones that were much bolder, ones he would quickly remove from Rozlyn before fucking her. But no matter what she wore, he would simply peel the fabric from her perfect body, revealing the delicacy that awaited him.

"Now this," he purred, "I like."

"Would you like to help me remove my clothing, so I may try one on for you?" She grinned.

Fuck. Yes. Haven's shadows seeped out of him, trailing their fingers up the curve of her waist, between her breasts to unfasten her dress. He teased them both while his shadows slowly removed her garments. With a snap of his fingers, his clothing vanished, making Rozlyn smile even more.

"You're so efficient," she drawled.

His lips claimed hers, tasting her alluring sunshine. He cradled her close and took her with him in a heap on the floor before rolling her to her back to graze kisses down her throat. His shadows caressed her thighs as he flicked his tongue over a peaked nipple and took it into his mouth. She moaned and he brought his lips to hers once more, yearning to kiss her for eternity.

"Marry me," he rasped, his eyes hooded. "Be my wife again."

Rozlyn stilled, her heart racing against his chest, her eyes dancing in excitement. "Yes! *But* only on two conditions. I want Iseult to initiate the ceremony. And!" She held up a finger. "Allow me to make your wedding attire!"

Haven chuckled. "I'll make arrangements as soon as you pick the date." Since Iseult was the ferryman, he could no longer cross into another court, but Haven would have his prior assistant stand on one side of the border between Souldark and Dawnbreak during the ceremony while Rozlyn's brothel family remained on the other.

"I'll even wear a black gown for you." She winked, then gripped his cock, and he released a groan of pleasure.

Rozlyn stroked him at a deft pace. *His Rozlyn.* Haven rolled with her to his back, and she cradled his thighs— he needed to feel her around his cock *now.* She slid down on him, making them both gasp.

Haven dug his fingers into her backside as she rode him, harder, faster, brilliantly. He kept his eyes open, studying her every feature, every curve, every movement. And he continued watching as her lips parted and her back slightly arched while discovering her own bliss.

His hands moved in sync with her body, her core grinding into him in the way that drove him mad, desperate for more. Closer. Closer. Until her name tore from his lips. "Rozlyn."

She collapsed against him, and he draped an arm around her waist, his chest heaving.

"I love you," he murmured. She'd spoken the words to him every day, and even though he felt the sentiment in return, he never said them aloud. They were words he'd never told anyone. Not his parents. Not Vivienne. No one. But he fucking loved her and wanted to give her everything.

Beaming like the sun, Rozlyn lifted slightly and kissed his lips. "And I love you." She dipped her head beside him, her soft lips brushing his ear as she whispered, "Now, let me measure you so I can get started on your attire."

Haven laughed and held his arms out for her. "As you wish."

Did you enjoy Tower of Shadows?

Authors always appreciate reviews, whether long or short.

Want to read about another Wicked Villain? Try Spindle of Sin!

Welcome to the dark world of Grimm, where the villains are as wicked as their desires.

Aura was always destined to become the Starnight Prince's bride following her twenty-first birthday. Now that the day has arrived, she looks forward to wedded bliss—and their first night together as husband and wife.

That is, until the savage dragon king from another court steals Aura away before the ceremony.

Hellbent on revenge, the King of Sin has been making careful plans to ruin the Starnight Prince. For years, he used lustful dalliances to battle his rage and bide his time. With Aura in his possession—the key to his vengeance—he'll use her however he sees fit.

But whenever Aura is near, the King of Sin wants nothing more than to unlock her inner desires, make her crave his touch and long for the pleasure only he can give.

No matter the sin. No matter what is to become of her.

ALSO FROM CANDACE ROBINSON

Wicked Souls Duology
Vault of Glass
Bride of Glass

Marked by Magic
The Bone Valley
Merciless Stars
Her Cruel Dahlias

Cruel Curses Trilogy
Clouded By Envy
Veiled By Desire
Shadowed By Despair

Untamed Darkness
And Then There Was Silence
Dearest Clementine: Dark and Romantic Monstrous Tales
These Vicious Thorns: Tales of the Lovely Grim
Savage Delights: Two Dark Tales

Cursed Hearts Duology
Lyrics & Curses
Music & Mirrors

Between the Quiet
Hearts Are Like Balloons
Bacon Pie
Avocado Bliss

ALSO FROM AMBER R. DUELL

The Dark Dreamer Trilogy
Dream Keeper
Dark Consort
Night Warden

Forgotten Gods
Fragile Chaos

Faeries of Oz Series
Lion (Short Story Prequel)
Tin
Crow
Ozma
Tik-Tok

Darkness Series: Temptation
Darkness Whispered

The Prince's Wing
When Stars Are Bright

Vampires in Wonderland Series
Rav (Short Story Prequel)
Maddie
Chess
Knave

Once Upon A Wicked Villain
Spindle of Sin
Tower of Shadows

Acknowledgments

The Grimms' Fairy Tales have such inspiring stories, and we of course couldn't deny a Rapunzel retelling! We wanted to write a story where Rapunzel wasn't entirely bound to a tower, and how there was more to her story as well as the villain who trapped her. We hope you enjoyed it, beautiful readers!

To our families and friends, after so many books, we still don't know what to properly say, but we love you. To Amber H. for being so incredibly helpful as always. Jerica for how you thoroughly find incredible fixes. To Lindsay, Hayley, and Ann, you guys are simply wonderful!

Since our Rapunzel retelling has drawn to an end, our next lovely villain you can find in our upcoming Red Riding Hood tale!

About the Authors

Candace Robinson spends her days consumed by words and hoping to one day find her own DeLorean time machine. Her life consists of avoiding migraines, admiring Bonsai trees, watching classic movies, and living with her husband and daughter in Texas—where it can be forty degrees one day and eighty the next.

Amber R. Duell was born and raised in a small town in Central New York. While it will always be home, she's constantly moving with her husband and two sons as a military wife. She does her best writing in the middle of the night, surviving the daylight hours with massive amounts of caffeine. When not reading or writing, she enjoys snowboarding, embroidering, and snuggling with her cats.

9 781960 949417